Chapter 1

BOOOOOMM!!!!

The bomb blast was two streets away, but it shook the pavement beneath our feet as my Aunt Abbey and I stumbled through the entrance of Mornington Crescent Underground Station.

"That nearly got us," I said as we made our way down the circular staircase, holding onto the handrail in case another explosion came. There had been nights when we'd been deep below ground here, when even the tube platform seemed to shake if a bomb was particularly close.

I'm Violet Debuchy – French name from a French father but an English mother – 17 years old, and right now doing my best to keep me and my aunt alive during the latest German bombing attack.

"I'm sure they've started bombing earlier tonight," said Aunt Abbey. "Or maybe the siren didn't go off properly."

"It went off, but you were hanging around looking for your ration book," I reminded her.

"It doesn't do to leave your ration book lying around in your house," retorted Aunt Abbey, following me down the winding stairs. "What if there'd been looters and the house had got blown up and they'd gone in and taken it?"

I was on the point of snapping back that if our house was bombed, a missing ration book would be the least of our worries, but I bit my lip to stop myself saying anything. Aunt Abbey may have her irritating ways, but then so have I. And Aunt Abbey had taken me and my parents in and given us a roof over our heads when we needed it.

We reached the station platform, which was already full. Some families had turned their particular spaces into underground homes: mattresses, chairs – with some using small paraffin stoves to boil a kettle to make a pot of tea. Other people had even built bunk beds for their children to sleep on.

"Hello, Mrs Hicks!" called our neighbour, Dolly Mason. "I've kept you and Violet a space!"

And she had, laying cushions out next to her patch of platform.

We sat down on the cushions.

"I'm sure the bombing's started earlier tonight," said Dolly Mason.

"That's what I said to Violet," nodded Aunt Abbey, and she and Dolly proceeded to engage in one of their regular conversations in the deep-underground air-raid shelter, while I did my best to let the situation wash over me. It'd be best if I could sleep, that's what Aunt Abbey always said to

MY STORY
CODENAME
CÉLINE

JIM ELDRIDGE

SCHOLASTIC

While this book is based on real characters and actual historical events,
some situations and people are fictional, created by the author.

Scholastic Children's Books,
Euston House, 24 Eversholt Street,
London NW1 1DB, UK

A division of Scholastic Ltd
London ~ New York ~ Toronto ~ Sydney ~ Auckland
Mexico City ~ New Delhi ~ Hong Kong

First published in the UK by Scholastic Ltd, 2015

Printed and bound in the UK by CPI Group (UK) Ltd, Croydon, CR0 4YY

2 4 6 8 10 9 7 5 3 1

www.scholastic.co.uk

me. But how could I sleep with bombs raining down around us, the tube station, the walls, the ground shaking with every new explosion, and the threat of everything coming down on top of us?

It was January 1944 and the War had been going on for four and a half years, since September 1939. That was the year when I – then 13 years old – had been brought to England from France by my dad and mum. Sometimes, when I close my eyes, I can still see my dad, Jacques Debuchy, coming home from work to our apartment in Paris and telling me and Mum: "The Germans are going to invade. Nowhere in France will be safe. Nor Belgium, or Holland. The Germans will sweep across border after border, just as they did in 1914. We have to leave."

And so we came to London, where my mother, Mary, had an older sister, Abbey. Abbey was a widow, and was delighted to welcome us into her home. "This house is too big for me since Henry died," she said. "It will be wonderful to have you staying here. You can stay as long as you like."

"There's a war coming," Dad had said. "We could be here for a long time."

"Everyone's saying if there is a war, it'll be all over by Christmas," said Aunt Abbey. "No one will want to go through again what we went through before. It's only twenty years since the last war ended!"

But within a month of us arriving in London, war had come.

At the start of the war, most of London's schoolchildren had been evacuated to the countryside, in expectation of air raids. I didn't go with the rest of the children because I'd only recently arrived in England, so I wasn't attached to any school. But after a month or so, when there had still been no signs of any air attacks on London, most children returned to the capital.

London's schools re-opened, and I was sent to the French Lycée, where most French families living in London sent their children, and where lessons were carried out in both French and English.

Despite growing up in France, English wasn't a problem for me. I'd spent a lot of time in England as a child, staying with Mum's family: her parents, Grampa and Granma; my Aunt Abbey and her husband; and Mum's handsome and funny younger brother, Eric. Lovely, wonderful Uncle Eric.

During the first months of the war, life had gone on much as normal. Like everyone else, I carried a gas mask with me wherever I went in case of an air attack by gas bombs. And at night all the streetlights were left unlit and heavy dark blackout curtains were pulled across windows to stop any light escaping that could help guide German bomber pilots to their targets: the cities. But then, in 1940, everything fell apart.

Uncle Eric, so dashing and great, was killed at Dunkirk, where half a million British and French soldiers had been forced back to the French coast by the Germans. Over 300,000 of them were rescued from the beaches at Dunkirk by the Navy, but thousands died or were taken prisoner. Uncle Eric was one of those killed.

Granma died soon afterwards, some said of a broken heart at the loss of her beloved son. And Grampa, aged 60, died soon after that of a heart attack.

Then, worst of all, in September 1940 came the Blitz – a series of air attacks night after night when the German Luftwaffe rained bombs down on London. Buildings were smashed to bits and the casualty rates rose rapidly. Thousands died. Among them was my mum. I can still hardly bear to think about it.

Mum had decided to stay the night with an invalid aunt of hers, Aunt Peggy, who was seriously ill. Aunt Peggy's house took a direct hit. Aunt Peggy, her family, and Mum were all killed.

Dad was in France when Mum was killed. In May 1940, soon after the Germans invaded France, he'd gone to join the French Resistance. He came back to England for Mum's funeral, but left soon afterwards, going back to France to carry on the battle. It was as if Mum's death had robbed him of all feelings except revenge.

He'd hugged me closely to him the last time I'd seen him,

before he'd returned to France, and whispered fiercely to me: "I shall pay them back for what they've done, ma petite!"

Since that day, in 1940, I hadn't heard a word from him. Almost four years! I knew it would be difficult for him to get a message out, but it was still hard not knowing if he was alive or dead.

I carried on with my life – living with Aunt Abbey, going to school at the Lycée – until I turned sixteen in 1942. Then I left school to go to work, as most others did.

My first aim had been to join either the Women's Royal Army Corps (the WRACS) or the Women's Royal Naval Service (the Wrens), but I was told at the recruiting office that I was too young. "Eighteen, dear," the woman had told me. "Then you can apply."

And so I'd looked for something else I could do that would help the war effort. I thought of nursing, helping the wounded, but I was told that I'd have to do two years' training. Two years! The War could be over by then!

The thing was that I wanted to be in action, which is why I'd tried to get into the WRACS or the Wrens. But then I found out that women in those services didn't actually see any action: their roles were restricted to cooks or messengers. I wanted to do something to pay the Germans back for killing my mum and Uncle Eric!

The Labour Exchange offered me a job in a munitions factory. "You'll be making bombs. That'll help the war effort." But there were problems with my papers. I was a French citizen, an alien. And the Government were rounding up foreign aliens.

"But my father's fighting the Germans in France!" I protested. "My mother and her family are English, and my mother was killed by the Germans! I live here! I'm English on my mother's side!"

"But you're French according to your birth certificate," said the woman at the Labour Exchange. "You were born in France."

And so I'd ended up working in a series of shops while I waited for my eighteenth birthday to come around. Then I'd be able to apply for the WRACS or the Wrens again. Even being a messenger would be doing *something*. I'd be in uniform and helping the fight.

I thought of trying to get into the WAAF, the Women's Auxiliary Air Force, working in the control rooms. I might even get to fly a plane! I knew there were women flying Spitfires, and even Lancasters, moving them from airfield to airfield. But, as with the other services, I was told I was too young.

So right now I'm a 17-year-old, living with my aunt, working in a clothes shop by day and spending most of my nights in the air-raid shelter deep underground, like now, and desperately wondering where Dad is, and what he's doing. Does he ever think of me? Does he miss me as much as I miss him?

Every night I say a silent prayer: Oh, Daddy, send me a note, a letter, a card, anything, to let me know you still remember me. But nothing comes.

....

Next morning, at dawn, Aunt Abbey and I made our way out of the tube station and headed for home. Every time we came up from below ground, I wondered if this would be the time we'd find our house gone, just like Aunt Peggy's house. But no, it was still intact, having survived the night's bombing. Many of the other buildings we passed hadn't been so lucky. Simmonds' Furniture Store, just round the corner from Aunt Abbey's house, had been completely demolished and was now just a massive tangle of smashed brick and roof tiles, broken wood and shattered glass. With the support of the furniture store's walls at each end gone, the interiors of the houses on either side were exposed – living rooms, bedrooms, kitchens – wallpaper torn and furniture blasted and wrecked, like ruined dolls' houses.

"That's Mrs Harrison's," said Aunt Abbey. "At least we know she wasn't in there."

Mrs Harrison and her family had been further along the platform on the Underground.

The house at the other side of the bombed-out furniture store looked as if it was about to collapse.

"Miss Yardley's," commented Abbey sadly. "She's lived in that house for seventy years. She was born in it." She frowned. "I didn't see her in the station last night."

"No, she's in hospital," I said. "Pneumonia. Her daughter told me."

Aunt Abbey shook her head sadly.

"When she hears about her house, that'll be it. All her memories are in that house. She'll give up the ghost, you'll see."

We turned the corner into our street and reached the front door just as the postman was arriving.

"Morning!" he greeted us cheerfully. "Not too bad last night!"

"Simmonds' Furniture Store was hit," said Aunt Abbey. "We just came past it."

"Hopefully there was no one in it," said the postman. He held out two envelopes. "One for you, Mrs Hicks, and one for you, Miss Debuchy. Official, by the looks of it." He winked. "Could be your call-up papers."

I took the envelope and saw the words "War Office" printed on the back in big letters. I felt a surge of excitement. Could it be my call-up papers? Perhaps the authorities had decided they couldn't wait until people got to the age of 18 any more before bringing them into the services. After all, there was war on and they needed every able person they could call on if the Allies were going to win.

I was already opening the envelope as I followed Aunt Abbey into the house. I took out the letter, typed neatly on official War Office headed notepaper, and read it. The words swam in front of my eyes as the tears came quickly.

"Dear Miss Debuchy.

We regret to inform you that your father, Jacques Debuchy, has been reported killed in action in France.

Please accept our sincere condolences.

Yours sincerely ...."

Chapter 2

I didn't reach the signature. I dropped the letter on the hall carpet with an agonized howl of anguish and slumped back against the wall, doing my best to stop myself from collapsing to the floor.

Aunt Abbey scooped the letter up and read it, then turned to me, her eyes also filling with tears.

"Oh no!" she exclaimed.

She dropped the letter back on the floor, and took me by the shoulders, lifting me away from the wall, and holding me tight.

"My dear Violet!"

"I never got the chance to tell him I loved him," I sobbed.

"Yes, you did. You told him before he went to France that last time."

"That was over three years ago!"

"And he would have kept that in his heart."

"Then why didn't he write to me?" I begged her.

"He was with the Resistance," said Aunt Abbey. "It's not easy to get a letter out. In fact, it would have been dangerous if he'd tried."

11

I bent down, picked up the letter and read it through again.

"It doesn't say how he died," I said.

"He was behind enemy lines," Aunt Abbey said again. "They possibly don't know."

"They must know!" I burst out. "If they know he's dead, they must know how he died!"

"It's the War Office," said Aunt Abbey. "They have to be careful what they say."

She bent down and picked up the envelope from the floor and frowned.

"There's something else in the envelope," said Aunt Abbey. She reached in and took out a small piece of paper. "It's a handwritten note, addressed to you." She peered at it. "From someone called Edward Swinton."

I took it from her and read the neat handwriting.

"Dear Violet.

I worked with your father. If you would like to talk about him, and learn more about what he did, please come to this address and see me.

Yours sincerely,

Edward Swinton."

Beneath was an address: Norgeby House at 64 Baker Street.

....

An hour later, I was standing outside Norgeby House in Baker Street, not far from the Underground station. I'd walked from Mornington Crescent, through Camden Town, then Regents Park. I noticed how the bomb damage became less noticeable the further I walked from Aunt Abbey's house. People said this was because the Germans were concentrating their bombing on the area around the three main railway stations: Euston, King's Cross and St Pancras, to disrupt railway traffic. Mornington Crescent was close to all three.

Aunt Abbey had cautioned me against going to see this Edward Swinton so soon.

"You've only just learnt of your dad's death," she said. "You need time to recover."

"This man may be able to tell me what the letter doesn't," I replied. "What he was doing. How he died. I need to know."

"You can go tomorrow."

"I need to know *now*," I insisted.

I had a quick wash to take away the smell of the Underground station air-raid shelter that hung around me, then set off.

Norgeby House was a large redbrick building, undamaged by any bombing, although the windows of the bottom two floors had metal grilles over them as a form of protection against flying debris from bomb blasts. A brass plaque by the main reception door said: "Inter-Services Research Bureau".

I went to the door and opened it, and found my way barred by a very large man in a tight-fitting dark suit.

"Sorry, admission by appointment only," he growled.

"I have an appointment," I said. Alright, strictly speaking that wasn't true, but I'd been invited.

"Who with?" demanded the man.

"Edward Swinton."

The man surveyed me carefully, then held out his open hand.

"Let's see your appointment card."

"I don't have one. He sent me a note inviting me to call on him here."

I took the piece of paper from my pocket and held it out to the man. He took it, read it, then gestured towards a desk with the sign "Reception" over it.

"Over there."

I took the piece of paper back from him and walked to the Reception desk. A blonde woman in her thirties behind the desk looked at me quizzically.

"Can I help you?" she asked.

"I'm here at the invitation of Edward Swinton," I told her. Once more, I produced the piece of paper and handed it to the blonde woman. The woman read it, then handed it back.

14

"Your name?" she asked.

"Violet Debuchy."

The woman lifted up a telephone handset, cranked a handle and, when the person at the other end answered, said: "I have a Violet Debuchy to see Mr Swinton." She listened for a moment, then replaced the phone.

"William!" she called.

Immediately, a man appeared from an inner doorway. Like the man in the dark suit on guard at the main door, he was large and very muscular, and I was sure I spotted the outline of a gun bulging through his jacket, just below his armpit.

"Take Miss Debuchy to Mr Swinton's office."

The large man nodded and gestured for me to follow him.

Two large men, both big enough to fit nicely into a rugby scrum, and one of them possibly armed with a gun. What sort of 'research' went on at this 'Inter-Services Research Bureau' I wondered.

The big man led me through a series of doors, and then down two flights of concrete stairs to a basement corridor. We passed along the corridor. All the doors in the corridor were shut and there seemed to be very little noise coming from behind any of them. Finally, we reached a door with the number '7' on it. The big man knocked at it, and when a man's voice from inside called: "Enter!", he opened the door.

"Violet Debuchy, Mr Swinton," he announced, and stood

aside to let me enter, then pulled shut the door behind him and left.

Edward Swinton stood up as I walked towards his desk. He was a small, very thin man in his forties, I guessed. Clean-shaven, his hair short and dark but turning grey. His clothing was very neat: a dark suit and what looked like a regimental tie. It struck me that he was a military type.

"Thank you so much for coming," he said, his voice sad. "I can only repeat my condolences at your dreadful loss." He gestured at the chair opposite him. "Please, do sit down."

"Thank you," I said.

I sat, and as he sat down, I said: "Your note said you knew my father."

"Yes," nodded Swinton.

"How?" I asked.

Swinton hesitated, his eyes searching my face as if looking for something. Then he said: "I'll come straight to the point, Violet. You don't mind if I call you, Violet, do you?"

"No," I said. "Violet is fine."

"As I said in my note, I worked closely with your father. He was a wonderful man."

"Yes," I nodded. "He was." I frowned and looked at Swinton quizzically. "When you say you worked with him, what does that mean, exactly?"

"A good question," nodded Swinton. "But before I answer, I must ask for your promise that nothing that passes between us will be repeated by you outside this office. Not even to your aunt, and certainly not to any of your friends."

"I promise," I said.

"Thank you," said Swinton.

I smiled. It was the first smile I'd been able to raise since I'd got the letter, but it wasn't a real smile – more of a suspicious smile.

"You take my word very easily," I pointed out to him. "Do you believe it every time someone says they promise?"

"Your father told me that if you gave your word, you meant it," said Swinton. "He said that you were absolutely to be trusted."

As Swinton said these words, I could feel tears pricking at the back of my eyes at the thought of Dad talking about me in that way. Don't cry, I warned myself. Dad wouldn't have wanted that.

"He was very proud of your achievements at school, both academically and particularly in sports," Swinton continued. "He said you were the bravest person he knew. He was particularly proud of you scoring the winning goal in a game of hockey for your school, even though you'd broken your arm a moment before."

"It wasn't actually broken," I corrected him. "Just chipped a little."

"He also said you could keep a secret like no one else. And what I'm about to tell you is a very big secret. If you don't feel you can keep it, then we'll just end this meeting very politely and you can go on your way."

Oh no we won't, I thought fiercely. This man knows something special about Dad, and I'm determined to find out what it is.

"I've already given you my word," I said, finding it hard to keep the annoyance out of my voice.

Swinton smiled again.

"You're very like your father, you know," he said. "He was always straight to the point, and he didn't suffer fools gladly, either."

His friendly manner made me relax a little.

"I'm sorry," I apologized. "I didn't mean to suggest I thought you were a fool …"

And I could tell he wasn't.

"Then let's get to it," he said. "Your father was a key part of SOE – the Special Operations Executive – which was set up by our Prime Minister Winston Churchill to fight the Nazis behind enemy lines."

"I knew he was fighting in France with the Resistance."

"Jacques was much more than that. He was a key organizer of the Resistance in northern France, and the liaison between the French Resistance and SOE's London headquarters." He smiled again. "Which is here, in this building."

"The Inter-Services Research Bureau?" I queried.

Swinton shrugged.

"It's a title that means nothing, and at the same time means exactly what it says: it brings together different services. In this case, spying, assassinations, explosives and saving lives."

I said nothing, but let myself take it all in. Spying? Assassination?

"SOE has agents in various countries occupied by the enemy: Greece, France, Italy, Holland, even Germany itself. My job as Head of F Section is with France. We prefer to use agents who have a French connection, especially those who are half-French and bilingual, because they can pass as French much more easily than an English person pretending to be French, no matter how good their French is."

"People like my father."

"And like you. Which is why I invited you here. How would you feel about becoming an agent, operating behind enemy lines in France?"

I stared at him, stunned. Me? Actually physically fighting the Nazis in this war! What was it he'd said? Assassinations! Explosives!

Swinton must have seen my astonishment in my face. This couldn't be happening! I was a girl, not long out of school.

"Before you say anything, I must warn you that it is very dangerous. Very dangerous indeed. There is a great risk of being captured by the Nazis, and the Gestapo are not gentle in their methods of extracting information, regardless of gender or age. A young woman is as at much risk as a young man, possibly more so …"

But I didn't need to hear any more. This was the opportunity I'd been waiting for, but one I thought only happened in dreams. I was suddenly scared that Swinton might change his mind and decide that I was too young after all, so I blurted out: "Yes! I'll do it!"

Swinton was studying me carefully.

"I am not exaggerating when I say it is dangerous. You could be killed. Unfortunately, the chances of that are very high …"

"I said yes and I meant it!" I told him firmly. "I've been desperate to do something for the war effort, but the only thing I've been offered as a woman is working in a shop! There are the services – Army and Navy – but again the women are kept away from the action, typing and passing messages around. This will be doing something real!"

And a chance to carry on Dad's work, I promised myself.

"The reason I would caution you is that you are still very young…," continued Swinton.

"In a few months I shall be eighteen," I replied. "That's the same age as the young men who are joining up to fight."

Swinton nodded.

"Very well," he said. "Welcome aboard! I'll fix up your

training – it's very intensive, but absolutely vital. The lessons you learn during training will help to keep you alive when you're out in the field.

"The important thing to stress again is absolute secrecy; officially, SOE does not exist. You will not be able to tell anyone about your work or this organization, not even your closest friends or relatives."

"Why?" I asked. "Aunt Abbey and I knew that Daddy was working behind enemy lines in France."

"You knew that he was a member of the Resistance," said Swinton. "You did not know that he was a member of SOE. Officially, SOE doesn't exist."

"Why?" I asked again.

He hesitated, then said: "Let's just say it's politics. Your official cover story will be that you have been offered a secretarial job with the Inter-Services Research Bureau, which co-ordinates paperwork. Your job will involve having to "go away to conferences to take notes". That'll be your cover story when you are away at training, and also when you're on a mission.

"As I said, officially, SOE and its agents do not exist. All our agents are given new names, new identities for when they are active. If they are caught, their true identities are not to be revealed. While you are on active duty – which includes your period of training – you will be Céline LeBlanc. It's not just a case of having new identity papers, you must become

Céline LeBlanc. You will learn how during your training." Swinton regarded Violet quizzically. "I am sure you have many questions you want to ask," he said. "I would ask you to keep them until after your training, just in case you change your mind."

"I won't," I said firmly.

"We shall see," said Swinton. "The training can be quite … tough."

"As my father said, I can be tough if needed," I retorted.

"We shall see," repeated Swinton. "There is a world of difference between playing hockey at school with a chipped bone and the kind of training you are about to be subjected to."

"I'll be up to it," I assured him. "But I do have one question: how did my father die?"

Swinton hesitated, then said: "He was captured by the Nazis and interrogated."

"Do you know who carried out the interrogation?"

"A Gestapo officer called Maximillian Schnell."

"The Gestapo?"

"Hitler's Secret Police. But they're not really that secret. They run everything in occupied France."

"And Schnell killed my father?"

"During the course of the interrogation."

I nodded.

"Thank you, Mr Swinton."

"Maximillian Schnell is a very dangerous man, Miss LeBlanc. You'll do your best to avoid coming into contact with him."

I nodded, but inside I promised myself I would have my revenge on this Maximillian Schnell. I looked forward to the day I came face to face with him.

Chapter 3

"How did you get on?" asked Aunt Abbey when I returned home.

"They offered me a job," I told her.

"A job?" said Abbey, surprised. "Doing what?"

"Secretarial work," I replied.

"But you can't type!"

"They'll teach me," I said. "But at first it's doing stuff like filing, putting papers in order."

Aunt Abbey frowned, uncertain.

"This has come a bit out of the blue," she asked suspiciously. "Who are they, this Inter-Services Research Bureau?"

"Oh, they're all very proper and above board," I assured her. "It's a Government Department responsible for keeping records. Not important ones, just the Accounts records of different departments, and things like that."

"But why did they offer it to you?"

I hesitated, and then decided that a part-truth was always more convincing than an out-and-out lie, which could be checked on and found to be a fraud.

"The man who put the note in the envelope telling us about Daddy, he turned out to be an old friend of his," I said. "I think he was feeling sorry for me and wanted to do something to help."

"I thought that letter came from the War Office," frowned Abbey suspiciously.

"They sent it on," I said, thinking quickly. "That's one of the things they do, this Inter-Services Research Bureau; they distribute post for different Government Departments. This man recognized Daddy's name in the official letter and put in a note of his own when he sent it out."

This explanation seemed to convince Aunt Abbey.

"Well that's a good thing," she said. "A job in an office will be much better for you than working in a munitions factory, or joining the Land Army. Much safer."

Secretly I thought: if only you knew!

"Yes," I said. "That's what I thought. He said I'd have to go away now and then."

"Why?"

"Well, to start with I have to be trained. So they're sending me on a residential course."

"For filing?"

"That, and also teaching me things like shorthand and typing."

"Surely you could go to a local college to learn those."

"Yes, but they like to do things their way." I gave her a

smile. "It is the Civil Service, after all."

"Yes, I suppose so," said Abbey reluctantly. "I'll miss you."

"I'm sure I'll be allowed time off to come home," I said, although I wasn't sure. Mr Swinton had talked to me for a long time, giving me more details and answering my questions, but I still wasn't certain what exactly lay in store for me.

....

It was two days later that a brown envelope arrived for me. Inside was a letter addressed to Céline LeBlanc instructing Céline to report to Cranleigh railway station in Surrey the following Tuesday.

"Please bring changes of clothing and toiletries for a stay of four days," the letter continued. "A railway ticket to Cranleigh station is enclosed. Make sure you catch the train that arrives in Cranleigh at 9.30am. A bus will be waiting to take you to your destination. The bus will have a card in its window saying 'Research Office'.

The following Tuesday I said goodbye to Aunt Abbey and caught the train to Cranleigh. The train was crowded, but I was lucky enough to get a seat. I was one of ten girls and women who got off at Cranleigh, all of us carrying luggage bags. Remembering Mr Swinton's firm instructions not to talk to anyone about SOE, or anything to do with it, I didn't exchange any words with the other girls, even though I guessed we were all quite likely there for the same reason. This was confirmed when every one of us headed for the cream single-decker bus that was waiting outside the station, each of us checking that it had a card with the words 'Research Office' in the window.

The driver stood outside, watching us, and seemed to be counting us as we got on the bus. When the last of us was on board, he climbed into the driving seat and switched on the engine.

I looked at the others. Three were about my age, late teenagers. Four looked to be in their twenties, and two were older, in their thirties. So far none of us had spoken, but once we set off the girl in the seat in front of me, who looked about seventeen, turned round and whispered excitedly to me: "I know we're not supposed to say anything, but isn't this exciting!"

I wanted to say "Yes", because it was, more exciting than anything I'd ever done before, but I was worried it might be a trap of some sort to see how loose-tongued I was. So instead I just whispered back: "You're right. I don't think we're supposed to say anything."

At this, she looked unhappy.

"But if we don't say anything, how will we know what we're supposed to be doing?"

"I'm sure we'll be told," I said.

I turned to look out of the window at the countryside as we passed, and also to avoid getting involved in any further conversations.

The bus climbed up and up, and I realized we were in the Surrey hills. The countryside around was green and beautiful, especially after the drabness of bomb-torn London. We travelled along a country road, then turned in at a wide gateway that had the name "Winterfold House" beside it, and continued along a winding drive. Through the trees and ornate rhododendron bushes I could see a large house emerging. No, more than a large house, it was a mansion.

"Wow!" breathed the girl in front of me in awed tones. "It's a stately home!"

As we rolled along the final stretch of the drive and pulled up outside it, I had to agree with her. It was a stately home, and I half expected a Duke and Duchess with lots of footmen and servants waiting outside to greet us, like in the films.

"All off!" called the driver.

We gathered up our bags and climbed down from the coach. A stern-faced woman was standing in the wide doorway of the house, at the top of a set of steps. She was holding a clipboard with a few sheets of paper on it. As we climbed the steps she gestured for us to go inside, with a terse: "Wait in the lobby."

The lobby, the reception hall, was like nothing I'd ever seen before in my life. If the outside was impressive, the reception area was awe-inspiring. There was ornate plasterwork on the cornices and ceilings, beautiful pastel shades of paint on the woodwork, exquisite Oriental-style wallpaper, and the walls hung with enormous portraits of people who were obviously very important and very rich, the paintings clearly stretching back a long way from the different fashions of costumes they wore.

As the ten of us newcomers gathered, I was aware of another ten women coming into the lobby from an interior door. Again, like our group, they were of mixed ages: some young, some older.

The woman with the clipboard came into the lobby and pulled the door shut.

"Welcome to Winterfold House," she said, her tone clipped. "It has been taken over for the war effort. The owners are still here, occupying a cottage in the grounds. Remember that we are their guests and while you are here you will be expected to treat this house, and the grounds, with respect.

"My name is Miss Penton and I will be your course leader. These girls ..." and she indicated the ten who'd just come from somewhere within the house, "are on the same course, but ahead of you. They're going to act as your guides for the first couple of days. You will each be allocated a room to share with one of them. They'll help you with any questions you may have. After you've been shown your room, leave your belongings there and come to Room 6, where we'll begin." She consulted the sheets of paper on her clipboard. "Josephine Barge!"

One of the older women in our group raised her hand.

"Me," she said.

"You will be with Marie."

One of the older women from the other group stepped forward and offered her hand to the woman who said she was called Josephine.

"I am Marie," she said. "Follow me."

The two went off together towards the stairs, and Miss Penton called out: "Annette Simenon!"

The girl who'd been sitting in front of me on the bus raised her hand, and another of the older women detached herself from the group and came forward to greet her. I was surprised – after the first pairing of the two older woman, Josephine and Marie, I thought they'd decided to match us by ages: young with young. I wondered who I'd be paired with.

I found out with the next call, as Miss Penton looked at her clipboard and announced: "Céline LeBlanc!"

I put up my hand.

"You're with Yvette."

A dark-haired girl of about my age came towards me,

smiling, and shook my hand.

"Yvette Debaille," she introduced herself. "Come with me and I'll show you to our room."

I picked up my small suitcase and followed her up the wide staircase.

"We'll only be sharing for a couple of days," said Yvette. "As Miss Penton said, our group are ahead of you, so we're off soon. Have you come far?"

It was asked so conversationally, so chattily, that I almost gave her the automatic answer of "Camden Town in London", before I remembered the instructions I'd been given: say nothing about yourself. Instead, I smiled, and said: "The journey was fine."

"The train wasn't too crowded, I hope," said Yvette. "Lately, every train just seems to be packed with men in uniform."

Again, I smiled and shrugged and said "It was fine."

By now we'd reached a door in the corridor, one of many, and Yvette stopped and said: "Here we are." She opened the door and I followed her in. It was a bedroom with two single beds in it, a dressing table, a low coffee table and a couple of chairs. The décor was old-fashioned: wallpaper with patterns of flowers, mostly pink.

"I can't stand this sort of wallpaper," shuddered Yvette. "It reminds me of my Granny's house. So old-fashioned!" She pointed to a door across the room. "We're lucky, this room has got an en-suite! Our own bathroom and toilet! Most of the other girls have to use the communal bathroom at the end of the corridor." She pointed to one of the beds. "That's yours. You have to make your own bed, and I'd advise doing it before you go down to breakfast in the mornings. They're very strict about order here." She laughed. "But what do you expect, it's a military place after all. That's why we're here."

Again, I didn't respond. Instead I put my suitcase on my allocated bed.

"Well, I suppose I'd better get along to Room 6," I said.

Yvette grinned and winked.

"Don't expect to have fun," she said. "Miss Penton is a real old sour-puss. Think about the strictest teacher you ever had at school, and double it. That's Miss Penton. Do you want me to show you where Room 6 is? This place is a bit of a maze until you get used to it."

"Yes, please," I said. It had already struck me that finding my way around Winterfold House was going to take some getting used to, and I didn't fancy getting lost for the first lesson. That wouldn't go down well with Miss Penton.

Chapter 4

The ten of us sat at our wooden desks in Room 6 and looked at Miss Penton, who stood in front of the blackboard and regarded us with a slightly disapproving expression. It was just like being back at school.

"Before we begin, I must impress on you the rules about security, not just while you are here, but ever afterwards.

"You will not be allowed to leave the grounds during the course unless accompanied or specially instructed to do so. You must never disclose at any time to anyone that you have been here, or at any of the other establishments you may attend. You must never recognize anyone who you have met here if you happen to meet them later elsewhere, except on official business.

"If you have promised to write a letter to anyone, it must be handed to me for censoring. You must not make any reference to that fact that your letters are censored.

"You will not be allowed to use the telephone here, or in the locality.

"Any breach of these rules will be viewed as a serious offence against the security of the nation."

Miss Penton looked at each of us in turn with a grim expression on her face, making sure her words had sunk in. Then, satisfied, her tone softened a bit as she continued: "With that out of the way, let me bid you welcome. I hope you will enjoy your course here and will find it helpful to you.

"I know you will be aware of this already, but we feel it's important for all new recruits to be reminded of the fact that this war is between us, the Allies – Britain, France, America, Russia, our Commonwealth countries, Australia, New Zealand, Canada, India – and the enemy, the Axis Powers: Germany, Italy and Japan. Here in F Division we concentrate on the situation in France, which has been under German occupation since the start of the War.

"The first aim of this organization is to damage the enemy's means of communication and production. The second is to strain the enemy's resources of manpower. The third is to undermine the morale of the enemy. If the morale of one side cracks, they lose the war, no matter how many troops they may have left in the field.

"The fourth is to raise the morale of the people in the countries occupied by the enemy, so that they will give us vital assistance when the right moment comes.

"How do we achieve all this? One word: sabotage."

I looked around me at the others sitting at their desks, and saw that, like me, all of them had suddenly become sharply attentive at this one word. This was what we were here for, to disrupt the German war machine, and ultimately destroy it.

For the next two hours, Miss Penton held us captivated as she drew diagrams and rough sketches in chalk on the blackboard, illustrating the impact of properly carried out sabotage behind enemy lines.

"Just think of the impact if it were possible to isolate the enemy's road and rail links, even for 24 hours, when the Allies are about to attack. It would be impossible for the enemy to get their troops to the threatened spot. The same applies to river bridges. Demolish a river bridge that is vital to the enemy's means of communication and troop movements, and the enemy will have to detour for miles, causing a delay of hours or, in some cases, days.

"Enemy telephone lines. Disrupt them, and the enemy have no way of communicating where urgent assistance or reinforcements are needed."

And so on, and so on; all of it gripping and making me want to be out there, in France, behind enemy lines, working with the Resistance, blowing up bridges and railway lines, cutting telephone wires.

One thing I learnt during the lecture that I hadn't known before: that the French Resistance was not just one organization, but two. The French Resistance consisted of people who outwardly carried on their daily lives, while at the same time carrying out acts of sabotage against the occupying German forces. The other organization, the Maquis, was made up of freedom fighters living in secret camps in woods and forests, and some high in the Alps and other mountainous areas. They dedicated their whole lives to attacking the Germans. Both the Resistance and the Maquis worked with SOE agents.

Finally, as the clock ticked to one o'clock, Miss Penton dismissed us for lunch.

"You will find the canteen at the end of the corridor. You are allowed to leave the house, but – I would remind you again – not the grounds. Be back here at 1.45."

The canteen was busy, mainly with men, I noticed. Some were in uniform, others in civilian clothes. There was no sign of Yvette, or the rest of the other group who had shown us to our rooms. What did grab the attention of all of us as we lined up with our trays at the buffet-style canteen service, was the wonderful quality of the food on offer.

"Look at this! Real meat! And proper potatoes!" burst out Annette excitedly.

"They've got their own small farm here," said Vivienne. "It's at the back of the house. I saw it from the window of my room. Vegetable plots and a chicken run. And pigs."

As I selected the different things to go on to my plate, I tried to remember when I'd last eaten something that looked as good and fresh as this. With the war had come rationing, with most food in short supply because attacks by German submarines, known as U-boats, had cut down the amount of food imported. Sugar had been one of the first things to vanish. Fresh fruit soon disappeared. Bananas were just a distant memory. Now and then apples were available, but not often, and not many.

Bread was also a problem because most of Britain's wheat had come from America and Canada. The German U-boats had put a stop to that, so the quality of bread we had was pretty horrible. Cheese was also scarce because there weren't enough cows in Britain to produce the milk to keep everyone supplied.

For most of us, especially those in the cities, we ate Spam – a kind of compressed meat which was supposed to be made from pork, but I had my doubts; and snoek – a fish which some said was made up of a mixture of whale meat and eels.

Eggs were another luxury. We were rationed to just one egg a week each, so most of the time things like 'scrambled eggs' were made from powdered eggs. My taste buds told me there were a lot of other ingredients in that powder than just eggs. The same was true of 'mashed potato', which was a powder mixed with water, and Aunt Abbey said tasted as much like real mashed potatoes as wallpaper paste.

People had told me that things were better out in the countryside, because people had gardens where they grew their own food, and if they were friends with a local farmer then they might be able to get hold of a piece of meat. From what Vivienne said she'd seen from her window, it sounded like it was true.

We sat down as a group at a long trestle table and tucked into the food in silence, savouring the flavours which we'd all been missing for so long and thought we'd never taste again.

After the main course there was apple pudding and custard, real pudding with real custard. Again, this was something that had become a distant memory.

"If this is how they eat in the SOE, I'm glad I joined up!" chirped Annette happily. Then she saw the looks of disapproval on the faces of some of the others, particularly the scowls from Lisbeth and Vanessa, and she looked unhappily embarrassed. But only for a moment.

"Well, we're all here together," she said defiantly. "Everyone knows why we're here."

"You still shouldn't say anything," reprimanded Vivienne sharply. "You need to get in the habit of shutting up."

Annette coloured.

"I thought we were supposed to be on the same side," she snapped back defensively. "I thought we were all comrades."

Vivienne didn't respond, she turned her attention back to eating her apple pudding. The awkward silence was broken by Natalie who said: "I'm getting a cup of tea. I think they might have real tea here, not just the dusty sweepings we usually have to put up with."

She headed towards a table where cups and saucers were

piled up next to a steaming metal urn of hot water, and some tea pots. Most of the others got up to go with her, leaving me to finish my pudding with Annette.

"It's not fair!" whispered Annette. "Everyone's ganging up on me." And I thought for a moment she was going to burst into tears.

Chapter 5

Back in Room 6, the afternoon lesson, again with Miss Penton, was something called Spycraft.

"The most important thing is you mustn't stand out," she emphasized. "Merge into the background. Not just in your behaviour, but especially in your clothes. Dress to fit. If you're going to be in Paris, dress like the women in Paris do. If you're in a country area, dress according to what local people wear. You'll find our wardrobe department is the absolute best. They'll be told which area to kit you out for, and what your cover is – whether you're an office worker, a student, whatever. You will *only* wear the clothes and shoes they give you. Do not take your own. We don't want you getting caught because your jacket has an English label on it.

"The same goes for hairstyles. Nothing fancy. Your hair will be cut and shaped to fit the local style.

"Language. You all speak French, which is why you've been selected, but beware of using phrases that could give you away as being from England, using everyday phrases you may have picked up living here. While you're in the field you mustn't just *speak* French, you've got to be *local*

40

French in every way."

And so on and so on. Those of us who'd been expecting something exciting and practical, like learning how to fire a gun, or how to blow up bridges, were disappointed. It was all about being lectured to. And we weren't allowed to take notes. Jeanine had asked if we could have some paper to make notes, but Miss Penton was immediately frosty.

"I would remind you of my words this morning about the importance of security. Written notes of things I tell you here would be in breach of that security. You might throw them away later in your room, and a cleaner could pick them up from a wastebasket. How do we know that cleaner isn't actually a spy, gathering vital evidence?"

And so we spent the afternoon committing the things we were told to memory, just as we had done that morning. By the time it came to bedtime, I was more than ready for sleep. Trying to remember everything Miss Penton told us, plus the fact that I hadn't slept properly the previous night because of the excitement of coming to this place, I couldn't wait to get into bed. But Yvette wasn't sleepy. She wanted to chat.

"Isn't this exciting?" said Yvette. "I've always wanted to do something like this!" She winked at me, conspiratorially. "So, what's your real name?"

I looked back at her, surprised.

"What?" I said.

"Oh come on!" she said, and she was grinning happily.

"We're all in this together!" She lowered her voice and whispered. "My real name's Susan! I'm not even French! Or even half-French! I suppose you're half-French. Most of the other girls are."

"We're not supposed to talk about ourselves," I pointed out.

"Yes, but that's in class, or when we're with the others!" She looked at me, conspiratorial again. "Come on, what's your secret?"

"I don't have one."

"Oh come on! Everyone's got secrets!"

"That's why they're called secrets," I said, which I thought was a clever reply and hoped it would shut her up.

It didn't.

"What do you think of Miss Penton?" she asked, changing tack.

I shrugged.

"She seems okay."

Yvette looked towards the door, as if worried there might be someone outside listening, and then whispered: "She's German! Her name isn't Penton at all! What do you think of that?"

Again, I shrugged as I started to get myself ready for bed.

"I don't think anything of it," I said.

"But you must!" burst out Yvette. "The Germans are our enemies! They started this war!"

When I didn't reply, she also began to get her pyjamas out of her bedside cabinet.

"Isn't this a fantastic place!" she sighed. "A real stately home! It's so different from where I grew up." There was a pause, and then she added. "Wigan. I grew up in Wigan. Do you know it?"

"No," I said.

"It's in Lancashire." She groaned. "Narrow grimy streets. It's a horrible place. What about you? I bet you were brought up somewhere grand. Somewhere posh. You *sound* posh."

I laughed.

"No one's ever called me that before," I said.

"Oh come on, they must have! Unless the rest of your family all talk like you do. Where do they come from? Some posh part of England, I bet." Then a thought obviously struck her, because she added. "Or some posh part of France!"

"We're not supposed to talk about ourselves," I reminded her.

"But there isn't anything else to talk about!" she groaned. "Oh, it's so *boring*!" She scowled. "If this is what being a spy's like, I don't think much of it."

"Is that why you're here?" I asked, pretending surprise.

"Of course! Isn't that why we're *all* here?" demanded Yvette. "That's what you're here for, isn't it?"

"I'm here to learn shorthand and typing," I said.

She shook her head.

"You are the weirdest girl I've ever met," she said. Then she changed her tone to one of gentle friendly pleading again: "Please, at least tell me your real name!"

I looked at the clock.

"I think I need to be getting some sleep," I said. "Another busy day tomorrow. Goodnight."

And with that I got into bed.

Chapter 6

When I woke the next morning, I was surprised to find that Yvette had already gone. What was more, her suitcase and clothes had all gone from the wardrobe as well. I could only imagine that she and the rest of her group were being moved somewhere else.

This feeling was confirmed when I arrived in the canteen for breakfast, and saw Josephine, Vivienne and Vanessa standing by one of the widows, and looking pretty angry about something.

"What's going on?" I asked as I approached them.

"That is," snapped Vanessa.

I looked out of the window and saw a parked coach, and Yvette and the rest of the women from the other group were getting on to it. But what was a bigger shock was that four of our group were also getting on board, and with their luggage: Annette, Jeanine, Claire and Diana.

"What's happening?" I asked, bewildered. "Where are they going?"

"Lucky people!" snapped Vivienne. "I bet they're being taken to the next stage of training, the real stuff! Guns and explosives!"

"But how come those four are going with them?" asked Vanessa indignantly. "I thought we all did okay yesterday!"

The same feeling about the unfairness of it struck me. Why had those other girls been selected to go wherever they were going, and not us?

I was still feeling upset about this when the six of us who remained – me, Vanessa, Vivienne, Josephine, Natalie and Lisbeth – filed into Room 6 for the morning's session. Miss Penton was standing by the blackboard, waiting for us.

"Take your seats," she ordered.

We sat down, and then, before I knew what I was doing, I put my hand up. The unfairness of the situation had got to me.

"Right …," began Miss Penton. "Today …" She stopped as she noticed that my hand was up. "Yes, Miss LeBlanc? You have a question?"

"Yes. Why have we been left behind? All the others are heading off somewhere, and pretty permanently by the look of it. They've got their luggage with them."

Miss Penton's lips tightened.

"You have obviously forgotten the first lesson yesterday, Miss LeBlanc," she said tersely. "You are not given information or explanations. The less you know, the safer it is for others, and for this organization."

I felt myself colouring with embarrassment, and mentally

kicked myself. Miss Penton was right; I'd just made a colossal error in asking the question. That's one black mark against my name, I thought bitterly. I've just pushed my chances of getting into action right back to square one.

Then Miss Penton's expression softened.

"However, in this case – and this time only – I will answer your question to allay any concerns the rest of you may have about whether you are suitable. The girls you saw leaving are going home. The girls you met yesterday to share with were SOE agents, one for each of you, to see how easily you would talk and gossip about yourself."

So that's why Yvette had been so chatty, I realized. It was a test!

"Four of your colleagues were deemed too loose-mouthed," continued Miss Penton. "They gave away too much information about themselves in friendly conversation, just because they thought the people they were talking to were safe. No one is safe. Something you mention in conversation to a friend or a relative, even in strictest confidence, can be passed on, even accidentally. Remember, careless talk costs lives." She picked up what looked like a small pack of postcards from her desk, and said. "Now the initial selection process has taken place, we can move on to the next stage."

With that she handed each of us a postcard, and a pencil. I wasn't surprised that Annette was one of those who'd gone. On the bus that had brought us from the station, she'd been bursting to talk about herself, and what we were going to do, so I was pretty sure that when she'd been offered the opportunity to talk, she'd done so.

I looked around at the five others left with me: Natalie, the other teenager; the two in their twenties: Vivienne and Vanessa; and the two older women, Lisbeth and Josephine. I wondered what other sort of traps there would be for us, and how many more of us would fail.

Miss Penton had returned to her desk. I picked up the postcard she'd given me. It was a picture of a small church by a village green. According to the title, it was a place called Binfield in Berkshire. I looked across at Natalie. Her postcard was a portrait of William Shakespeare. Beneath the picture was the caption: Stratford-upon-Avon.

"All of you have relatives or friends you were staying with before you came here, who will be expecting you to return shortly."

Miss Penton picked up a stick of chalk and wrote on the blackboard: 'Change of plan. I've been sent here for further training and some work that they say is vital for the war. I'll be in touch as soon as I've finished. Looking forward to seeing you soon.'

"Write this on your postcards, and address them to whomever is expecting you to return to them. Then give them to me and I will make sure they are posted in the right place.

"When you have done that, you are to return to your rooms, pack your bags, and meet in the reception area."

So we were moving. Where to? I wondered. I was tempted to ask Miss Penton, but I'd already learnt that would not be taken well, and I didn't fancy being sent home, as had happened to Annette and the others.

I wrote the card, addressed it to Aunt Abbey and handed it to Miss Penton. Six postcards, all with different place names on them. If anyone was hoping to get information about where we were headed next, they would be disappointed.

Chapter 7

Our transport this time was a black van, with room for five
people on each side on long wooden seats in the back. The
six of us climbed in, dumped our suitcases and bags on the
floor, and made ourselves as comfortable as we could on the
hard wooden seats.

"Wonder how long we're going to be travelling in this
thing?" asked Natalie unhappily, shifting on the seat.

"If you get uncomfortable, roll up your coat and use it as
a cushion," advised Vivienne.

With no windows to look out of, we had no way of
knowing where we were headed. There was a partition
between us and the van driver so we couldn't get a peek out
that way, and the rear windows of the van had been painted
over with black paint. It was all very hush-hush and secret.

We didn't talk much on the way. All of us were still very
aware of the four who'd been kicked off the course because
they'd been too loose-mouthed and talked too much about
themselves, and we were all worried that could happen to
us. After all, for all we knew, one of us could still be a plant,
reporting back about us. So our conversation stayed on

simple, uncontroversial things, like how bumpy the road was.

Finally, after about an hour, we felt the van begin to slow down, then pull to a halt. We heard the van driver's door open and shut, followed by footsteps on gravel, and then the rear door of the van opened.

"Out you come, ladies!"

We stumbled out of the van, feeling slightly cramped from the journey. A tall broad-shouldered man, in his late twenties, wearing blue overalls, stood smiling in welcome at us. I noticed that he had no badges that could identify him as military in any way, but I felt immediately that he was.

"I'm Harry, and I'm going to be one of your instructors," he said.

Lisbeth and I exchange sceptical looks. Harry? I could tell that, like me, she thought this wasn't his real name. Nothing about this business was what it looked like. Even our first day at Winterfold House had really been about weeding out the weak links, the ones who might give the game away.

"Follow me, and I'll show you where you're staying," he said.

We picked up our suitcases and bags and trudged behind him across the camp. It looked like a military base, with long single-storey wooden huts dotted around, and military vehicles of different sorts. But none of them had any markings on them.

A high wire fence ran all the way around the area, with

51

rolls of barbed wire at the top. I looked back and saw the main entrance – two tall metal gates that were shut. One thing was certain: we wouldn't be able to just walk out of this place.

Most of the other people on the base seemed to be men. Like Harry, they wore plain blue overalls rather than uniforms. Some were armed, rifles slung over their shoulders. Others were working on the different vehicles dotted around.

"Hey, look!" whispered Natalie.

I turned, and saw the ten women who'd been in the other group at Winterfold House, running together, not fast but hard. Their tops were grimy and soaked in sweat, and there was a look of grim determination on their faces. Two men, both wearing vests and shorts, ran alongside the women. I saw that Yvette was among the group and was tempted to give her a wave, but then I remembered what Miss Penton had said about not recognizing anyone you may meet while on the course.

The ten women and the two men thundered past us, arms and legs going, heads down.

"So that's what awaits us," muttered Vanessa.

"This way!" called Harry.

We continued across what I guessed to be a parade ground to one of the wooden huts. Harry opened the door.

"This is yours," he said.

We stepped in. Six metal-framed beds were in the hut, with sheets, blankets and pillows in a neat pile on top of the thin mattress on each. This was very different to the bedrooms at Winterfold House. Also on each pile was a blue overall.

"Toilets and washing block next door," said Harry. "It's ladies only, so you won't have to battle with any men for a washbasin." He gestured at the beds. "Make your beds and unpack, and put on the overalls. I'll be waiting for you outside."

With that, Harry left, pulling the door shut.

We looked at the beds.

"I'll take one farthest from the door," said Vivienne. With that she strode to the end of the hut and dropped her bag onto one of the two beds there.

"Shouldn't we draw lots?" suggested Natalie. "That would be fairer."

Vivienne gave her a cold glare.

"Life isn't fair," she said. "But I'll fight you for it if you like?"

Natalie looked back at Vivienne, not sure if she was joking. Then she shrugged. "Have it if you want. I don't mind which one I have."

I moved swiftly, joining Vivienne at the far end of the hut and dumped my suitcase on the other bed furthest from the door.

"If it's first come, first served, I'm grabbing this one," I said.

Vivienne looked at me and smiled.

"Good girl," she complimented.

We made our beds, and I was aware of how thin the mattress was. Sleeping on this for the next few nights would take some getting used to. I was going to be uncomfortably feeling the wires of the springs through it. But then it was the same for everybody. And if it got too bad, I could always spread my coat under the mattress.

We changed into the blue overalls and joined Harry outside.

"Right," said Harry. "We're going to start with some basic weapons training. Anyone used a gun before?"

Lisbeth, Vivienne and Josephine put their hands up, making me wonder in what sort of situation they'd each done that. I was even more intrigued when Harry asked: "Any of you fired a sub-machine gun?" and Vivienne and Josephine lowered their hands, but Lisbeth's stayed up.

Harry grinned at Lisbeth. "Good. One less to bother about when it comes to a weapon kicking back. Right, follow me."

As we walked, I wasn't the only one looking at Lisbeth with new respect, strongly tempted to ask her how and why she'd been firing a sub-machine gun. Harry led us to a large shed made of corrugated iron. Inside, another man was standing by a table on which a selection of guns was laid out: pistols, rifles, machine guns.

"This is Pete," Harry introduced him. "He knows more about weapons than most people will ever know. If you've got any questions and I don't know the answer, Pete will."

We looked at Pete, who just looked back at us, silent and unsmiling. He didn't look very approachable.

"Right," said Harry, gesturing for us to gather around the table. "We don't know what weapons you might be issued with for when you're in the field, so I'm going to run through the key ones, the ones you're most likely to be using. First, pistols."

From then, Harry showed us guns of all sorts: pistols, rifles and sub-machine guns. We picked them up and held them while he talked us through what they could do, how one sort was better than another, the different sorts of ammunition they used – everything about them. He showed us the difference between the revolvers, where the bullets were kept in a round chamber, and automatic pistols, where the ammunition was in a clip in the handle. He warned us about recoil, which meant a gun kicking back when it was fired.

Finally, he said: "So, ladies. We'll start with the easy ones first. Select a pistol each, and we'll go out to the firing range. Pete and I will bring the ammo."

Chapter 8

I selected one of the revolvers. I chose it because it reminded me of the guns they used in the cowboy films I used to go and see with Dad and Mum when I was a child in Paris.

The firing range turned out to be another metal shed. At the far end, dummy people made out of straw had been set up, tied to stakes. Large sheets of paper had been placed over their fronts. Behind the dummies, a thick wall had been built made up of wooden railway sleepers. I supposed this was to stop the bullets hitting the metal wall at the back, and either going right through it, or bouncing back towards the person who'd fired.

"Let's start one at a time," said Harry. "Collect your ammunition from the boxes over there. Make sure it's the right ammo for your gun. Lisbeth, you've shot before, so you can show the others how it's done."

Lisbeth went to the ammo box. Like me, she'd chosen a revolver. She expertly slipped the six bullets into the chamber, then walked to a line that had been painted on the floor opposite the target dummies. She didn't do anything fancy with it, just aimed the gun straight in front of her, arms straight but with a slight bend at the elbows, holding it in both hands.

Bang! Bang! Bang!

She fired three times. The first two shots hit the dummy in the centre of the chest. The third punched a hole in the paper covering its straw head.

"Good," nodded Harry. He turned to us. "Straight arm action, but with flexibility at the elbow to deal with the recoil, so no impact strain on the shoulders." He looked at Lisbeth. "Why two in the chest and one in the head?"

"The chest is the bigger target. You're more likely to get a hit there than the head. The head shot was vanity, to show I could do it."

Harry smiled.

"And why just three shots? Why not the whole chamber?"

"Always keep shots in reserve in case of trouble," said Lisbeth.

Harry nodded.

"Excellent!" he complimented her. "Yes, you've definitely done this before."

Where? I wanted to shout out. I was so eager to find out where Lisbeth had learnt to shoot like that, and why? But I knew I couldn't ask her direct.

Harry then called Vivienne and Josephine to the line to take their shots one after the other. They also kept their shots to three. I guessed they'd learnt from Harry's good reaction

57

to Lisbeth's display. Both of them hit the target, though Vivienne's shots were closer together.

"Céline," said Harry.

I selected six bullets from the ammo box and slipped them into the revolving chamber. I walked to the line, aimed the pistol at one of the dummies as Lisbeth had done, pulled the trigger … and nothing happened. I turned to Harry, puzzled.

"Sorry, Céline," he smiled. "I was hoping that one of you would do that, as an example to the others."

"Safety catch," said Lisbeth, Vivienne and Josephine in unison.

Harry came over to me and showed me where the safety catch was, and how to click it off so that the gun would fire.

"That's a vital lesson," he said. "You'd be surprised how many people forget about the safety catch, especially when they're in a tight situation."

I levelled the pistol at the dummy again, sighting along the barrel, and pulled the trigger.

The pistol kicked in my hand, the barrel jerking up, and the bullet sailed over and wide of the dummy and thudded into the wooden wall.

"Kick-back," said Harry. "Next time, squeeze the trigger more gently. And keep a tight grip of the handle with both hands, ready to force the barrel down at the very second of firing."

This time I overdid the forcing it down, and the bullet hit the dummy somewhere around what would have been the ankle.

"You hit it," nodded Harry. "That's a good start. Try again."

I fired again, but this time my shot missed the dummy altogether.

"Don't worry about it," said Harry, doing his best to reassure me. "It took me ages to get my eye in when I first started. Have another go. You've still got three bullets left. Might as well keep trying."

I tried again. My fourth shot missed the dummy again, my fifth took a piece of straw out of the side of the chest, bringing a mutter of "Better" from Harry; and then, to my delight, my last shot hit the dummy right in the chest.

"Excellent!" beamed Harry. "And this is your first time. Keep this up and you'll become a crack shot!"

I then moved away from the line to let Vanessa and Natalie have their turns. Like me, they missed with their first shots, but their other shots were closer and hit the target. I guessed they'd learnt from my mistakes.

We had one more round of pistol-shooting, and then Harry produced the Sten gun.

"Right, time for this one," he said. "And we'll start with single shot action so you can get used to the recoil. Two ways of aiming this: one, from the shoulder, like a rifle, taking careful aim. Two, from the waist. Which method you use depends on preference, and the circumstances. Lisbeth, you go first."

Lisbeth took the Sten from Harry, went to the ammunition boxes and took out a clip of bullets, which she clicked into place in the sub-machine gun. She seemed very comfortable with the weapon and the way it operated.

She walked to the line, put the butt of the gun to her shoulder and fired two single shots, which thudded into the dummy, ripping the paper. Then she switched the trigger mechanism to the "automatic fire" mark, dropped the handle to her waist, and let fly with a hail of bullets that tore the dummy in half, the bottom half falling to the floor.

"And that, ladies, is how it should be done," beamed Harry. He looked at Pete. "What do you think, Pete?"

Pete stood, silent, as if he was thinking it over, and then he shook his head and said, "Marvellous! Absolutely bloody marvellous!"

looking weapons: knives, clubs, guns, swords, even a wicked-looking spear.

"This is Bill," said Harry. He saw us looking at the weapons uncertainly, and grinned. "Don't worry. You won't have to sword-fight with one another."

And with that, he left.

Bill gestured for us to gather round him in a circle.

"Right, ladies, I'm going to be your instructor in unarmed combat. That means exactly what it says. You haven't got any weapons on you. Your gun's jammed, you've lost your knife, so your only weapon is you. And that weapon – the human body – can be devastating. You can kill or disable your opponent within seconds. Your primary weapons are your hands and feet. Elbows and knees are good, but they are joints, and if you crunch them into something hard, like a human skull, you can damage them and disable yourself."

As I stood there listening to him talking about deliberately hurting people – killing them – in such a matter-of-fact way, I realized how shocked I was. Not just by the extreme violence of what he was telling us, but by the fact that I was there listening, learning all this, and might have to use it. It went against everything I'd been brought up to think and believe, about being kind and caring to other people. And I realized that this is what war does. It changes people. It makes them brutal. I was being trained to kill people. To shoot them. Stab them. Kill them with my bare hands. But would I actually be able to do it?

And then I thought of Schnell, torturing my father to death, and the anger that filled me made me realize that if I ever met him, I could kill Schnell with no conscience.

Bill was still talking, explaining how to use our bodies as weapons. "Elbows and knees are fine when hitting soft areas – the groin, the stomach, the front of the throat – but for really effective damage, use your hands and feet as hard and fast as you can.

"For hands: either the fist, with the knuckles as the impact weapon, or the edge of the hand. And again, if you use the edge of the hand, it's the outside length of the little finger that is the weapon. It's hard because it's bony, and it has the other three fingers behind it to give weight to the blow.

"Next: targets. Places where your opponent is most vulnerable. If it's a man, the groin. A hard kick there will disable most men. The knees. Kick your opponent hard beneath the knee and you'll dislocate the kneecap. The pain is excruciating. And he won't be able to get up.

"Remember, when it's him or you there ain't no time for niceties. The longer he stays alive or conscious, the more danger for you. He'll kill you, so you've got to stop him. And quick. Because if he shouts, there'll be others coming, so you've got to finish him and get out of there quick."

And so on, until I became almost frightened at the thought of how easy it was for someone to kill another.

Finally, Bill said: "Right, that's the theory. Now, let's try it out. In pairs. You two …" pointing to me and Lisbeth "… one pair." He then put Natalie and Vivienne together, and then Josephine and Vanessa.

"At this stage, I want you to avoid actual contact with one another," he said. "You're too valuable to have you going off with a smashed windpipe at this early stage." He handed me, Natalie and Vanessa a knife each, and I realized that the blade was actually made of wood and painted silver. "Later on we'll be using the real thing, but at this stage … safety first."

We went through the processes and the actions under Bill's direction, our actions deliberately slow, almost like doing a mime play. Then we switched roles, Lisbeth the attacker and me the defender; and finally we each had a chance to attack Bill with whatever weapon we chose. Every time, Bill disarmed us, even when Vivienne chose a Sten gun. And not one of us got hit.

"But next time we'll have contact," Bill promised us.

I felt strange by the time we trooped into the Mess Hall for our evening meal. First the session on the firing range, then the unarmed combat practice. I suddenly realized I could do things with my body. Yes, I'd been pretty good at sports at school, but this was so much more, and so different! It was also frightening and shocking.

Over our meal we kept our conversation light, talking

about the day's events, the guns and the firing range and Bill and the unarmed combat session. We couldn't talk about ourselves without giving something away about who we really were, or where we were from – we were on our guard the whole time. In that way, it was good practice.

All the others in the Mess Hall were men, talking and laughing. We knew that there were many more men in SOE than there were women, and I wondered how many of them were training like us, and going on missions.

"Looks like the other group has arrived," said Josephine.

I looked towards the door and saw that the other group of women, with Yvette, had just come in and were heading for the food. Yvette saw me and came over, a smile on her face.

"Hi girls," she greeted us. She grabbed a nearby empty chair, moved it next to me and sat down. I saw that the others in my group were curious at this arrival, but they continued chatting together, although I knew that they would be half-listening to Yvette. As I would, in their position.

"I just wanted to come over and say I'm glad you made it," said Yvette. "All the time at Winterfold House when I was chattering away, trying to draw you out, I was hoping you wouldn't."

"Why?" I asked.

Yvette shrugged.

"Just a feeling," she said. "I think you've got what it takes to do this job."

Chapter 10

The next two days involved more weapons training, as well as introducing us to codes, secret inks and different sorts of disguises. Most of it, apart from the weapons training, took the form of lectures in a one of the wooden huts.

"This is just basic training," said Vanessa at the end of the day. "We won't get on to the good stuff until we're doing the proper course."

"What do you mean: the good stuff?" asked Natalie.

"Practical stuff. Explosives. Demolition. Assassination. Parachute jumping."

"How do you know?" asked Lisbeth.

Vanessa shrugged.

"I like to know what's going on," she said. "That's what gives you the edge in situations."

Vanessa's predictions of what lay in store for us were confirmed on the morning of our last day, when we trooped into the lecture room and found Edward Swinton waiting for us.

"Good morning, ladies," he said.

A quick look around at the faces of the others told me

that they all knew who he was, and had all met him before. As in my case, it looked like he'd been the one who'd recruited them.

"I'm pleased to inform you that you have all passed the selection process. The next stage will be full and proper training to prepare you for action in the field. That will begin in a week's time, so you will have time to spend at home with your families, those of you who have them.

"Again, I must stress that you cannot even hint to any of them what your real work is. And we will be monitoring you. We have agents everywhere, and if they hear even a whisper from your family or friends that you are engaged in any sort of spying or secret operations, you will be dropped.

"Now I know it's asking a lot of you to lie to your family and friends, people you are close to, but a slip could put a whole operation at risk. People's lives are at stake. The people you will be with in France are putting their lives at risk working with you. The Allies need you to succeed if we are to defeat the Nazis.

"You training will take about four months, at different locations. It will be in different aspects of your new trade. You've already had basic training. You will have further training in weapons and unarmed combat, as well as in fieldcraft, how to survive off the land, codes, radio communications, disguise, explosives and demolition, assassination techniques, and parachute jumping."

I couldn't resist a quick look towards Vanessa: everything he'd said was as she'd predicted. How did she know? Had she said it deliberately to see how we'd react? Was Vanessa a plant among us, an insider to watch us at close quarters and report back? Had she been looking for a reaction from us to her prediction about our future training, something she could report back?

Swinton handed each of us an envelope.

"Inside you will find a letter to you from the Inter-Services Research Bureau, addressed in your real name, instructing you to report to such-and-such a department for a period of four weeks as temporary cover. You can show this to your families to let them know why you will be going away. Each letter states a different location, just in case they fall into enemy hands, so there will be no co-ordination. You will also find a rail ticket to Cranleigh for next Wednesday.

"You will be met at Cranleigh station at 9.30am by a bus, as before. After one day at Winterfold House, you will spend time at a variety of locations on your final training. Providing that is successful, you will then be assigned your missions."

....

A few hours later we were packed up and bundled into the back of the same van that had brought us, and driven back to Cranleigh railway station. There, we caught the train back to central London and separated. There were no hugs, just waves of goodbye. We were a unit, almost comrades, but not close friends. It was as if the world we were being led into didn't allow us to have close friends. We were separate, from everybody.

Aunt Abbey was pleased to see me, and full of gossip about what had been happening locally. As I listened to her talk about what the neighbours had been up to, and how the local butcher, Mr Higgs, had managed to get hold of a leg of lamb, I felt distant from it all. Even though I'd been away for just a few days, the world I'd been exposed to was so far removed from this everyday life – even in war-time, with the bombing and the air-raid shelters – that I felt like a stranger.

Luckily, Aunt Abbey didn't notice anything different, or, if she did, she didn't say anything, and for the next week we settled back into our old routine: going out to the shops during the day, listening to the radio in the evenings, and spending a couple of nights in the tube station when the air-raid siren sounded.

Aunt Abbey was disappointed when she heard I was going to be away for four months – "Four months! The war could be over by then!" – but she was pleased when I showed her the letter Edward Swinton had given me.

"They obviously think a lot of you, dear," she said. "It sounds like an important job, and if you do well at it, who knows. There are always good opportunities for promotion in the Civil Service."

Chapter 11

A week later I said goodbye to Aunt Abbey and reported back to Winterfold House. To my surprise, only five of us caught the bus from the station – Josephine was missing. We were all aware of her absence, but none of us wanted to say anything about her. Ask no questions, that was the rule.

It was Miss Penton who filled us in when we gathered once more in Room 6.

"You will notice that there are now only five of you," she said. "I regret to inform you that the woman you knew as Josephine was killed in an air raid last week. Her death brings it home to us why it is so important that we bring this war to a quick resolution, and that is your job."

And that was it. Just a simple statement. Josephine was gone. All of us had lost people in this war, and almost everyone had lost someone *very* close. But none of us in this room were allowed to be close to each other. None of us even knew the real names of the others, or anything about their lives.

After that first day back at Winterfold House, the next four months were a blur as we were moved from base to base for different sorts of training. I was no longer Violet Debuchy, I was Céline LeBlanc. Many of our lessons were conducted in French to keep us constantly aware that we would be French people in France; we had to think in French. All of us, I noticed, slipped back into talking in French quite easily, and I became aware of our different accents: Vivienne had a Paris accent, similar to my own, while Natalie's was more southern France, and Lisbeth and Natalie had hints of Normandy.

Our course covered absolutely everything. As well as more involved unarmed combat and weapons training – including, as we'd been promised, learning to take a Sten gun apart and reassemble it blindfolded – we were give practical hands-on experience in radio communications, using explosives, sending messages using invisible inks and codes, disguise, fieldcraft, and what we might experience if we were caught and interrogated.

"The business of interrogation depends on the level of the person questioning you," we were told. "If it's just gossip and rumour that have led to you being questioned, then it may well be just at local level: the local French Police Chief. If so, it's important that you stick to your story: you are just an innocent person. Don't try and be clever, superior or blustering. Be upset, horrified, shocked at such a suggestion, but keep your reaction under control. Don't annoy your interrogator, try to keep on their side. You know they are only doing their job, that sort of thing. Upset them, and they might well hand you on to the Germans.

"Again, if it's just a German military bureaucrat, do the same: protest your innocence, but don't upset or annoy them. Try and persuade them the stories must have been spread by someone who doesn't like you for some reason, or it's a case of mistaken identity. Keep to your story: you are innocent.

"The problem comes if the Gestapo take you in for questioning."

Yes, I thought bitterly as I listened to the instructor, like Maximillian von Schnell with my father.

"The Gestapo are dangerous. The type of interrogator will change depending on the kind of person they think you are. Some will bully and threaten you. Others will appear to be gentle and kind, apologetic. Often they will mix the interrogators: first the bully, then the kind one, then the bully again. Sometimes they will put in an interrogator who seems really stupid and you think you can run rings round him. Don't try. These are often the most dangerous types, because they are waiting to see if they can trip you up.

"What they are after is not just you, they want the information you have: the names of the people you work with, and as much information as they can get from you about this organization. So they won't kill you right away. But they will, once they feel they've got everything out of you that they can.

"I have to tell you that, once you get into the hands of the Gestapo, we will be able to do little to help you. All you can do is stick to your story of innocence, and hope they believe you. If they don't, they will use every method at their disposal to get you to talk. That will include torture. It's only fair that you know this before you embark on a mission. You can still pull out."

None of us did. I had to admit I felt scared at the idea of being captured and tortured, scared to the point of feeling sick, but I'd come this far and I wasn't backing out now. I was going to do everything I could to make sure the Germans paid for what they did to my father, and to my mother.

Our final training was parachute jumping. For this we were taken to the Parachute Training School at RAF Ringway near Manchester. I had to admit this was the part I hadn't been looking forward to. I'd never been unduly worried about heights, but the idea of jumping out of a plane a couple of thousand feet high and relying on a piece of cloth to land safely made me very nervous. But to my surprise, I loved it! Hanging in the sky, learning to stay up for longer by manipulating the parachute, before landing was one of the most amazing experiences I'd ever known.

After parachute training, we were sent back home to await instructions. This was the hardest time for me. I was bursting to tell Aunt Abbey what I'd been up to the last four months, the incredible sense of power at being able to blow up a building, jump out of an aircraft, fire a machine gun, disarm an armed man with a kick and a chop of my hand, but I couldn't. And I so wanted to tell her that I would be going behind enemy lines to help win this War, and I'd be doing it for Dad and for Mum and for her and for everyone in the country, and the whole of Europe. But again, I couldn't say anything. Instead, I had to pretend to be lowly officer worker, Violet Debuchy, and chat away with her about mundane boring things, and pretend nothing out of the ordinary was happening for me. As we'd been instructed so many times: "You must never act in any way that makes people close to you wonder about you. Don't be secretive, or suddenly extra-gossipy, if that wasn't the 'you' before."

The trouble was that old 'me' had gone, and I knew I would never be her again.

Chapter 12

It was a fortnight after I returned from training that I received a letter from Edward Swinton summoning me to his office at Baker Street. At last! I thought, hoping that I would finally be going on a real mission.

Mr Swinton motioned me to a chair on the other side of his desk.

"I've heard good reports about you," he said.

"Thank you," I replied.

I waited.

"The instructors tell me you showed a real talent when it came to handling explosives."

I nodded in reply, but said nothing, waiting. Suddenly he laughed.

"Another thing you've got even better at is saying nothing," he chuckled.

"Trust no one," I reminded him.

He nodded, and then said in serious tones: "There's a railway bridge in Normandy we could do with blowing up. Think you can handle it?"

Blowing up a bridge! Real action! Although I did my best

to remain outwardly calm, inside I wanted to leap to my feet and give a shout of delight.

"Yes," I said, keeping my voice cool.

Swinton took a map from a drawer in his desk and unfolded it on a table. It showed the area of Normandy in northern France.

"You're going to Malerme, a small village just outside Caen," he said. "The good news is that you won't have to drop by parachute. The local Resistance have got a couple of fields they use for getting things in and out, and we have the ideal plane for the job: a Westland Lysander, a lovely little machine."

"What's the bad news?" I asked.

"The area is crawling with Germans. A lot of their big guns and heavy tanks are based at Caen, so security is tight across the whole area. Constant patrols. That's one of the reasons you won't be parachuted in, there's too big a risk you'll be blown off course and land where the Germans are.

"Because of the patrols, we won't know exactly which field you'll be dropped in. The pilot will head for the general area, and the locals will light signal fires to guide him in."

"Won't the Germans spot the fires?"

"The Resistance dig holes in the ground, four of them to form the corners of a box shape, and put wood and paraffin in them. When they set the fires they can be seen from the sky, but not from the ground. Once the plane's down, they shovel earth in the holes, which puts the fires out." He smiled. "They know what they're doing."

"And this bridge?" I asked.

Swinton pointed to a river on the map that meandered and snaked through the countryside. A railway line crossed the river.

"This railway line is the main one transporting German troops and weapons to their defences on the Normandy coast. Ideally, we'd like it destroyed by the fourth of June."

"I'll do it!" I said.

"Good," Swinton smiled. "In that case, I'll make the arrangements. Get you fixed up with the right sort of clothes, your documents. I've been looking at your record. You spent some time in Rouen?"

"As a child," I nodded. "My father had an aunt there we used to visit."

"You know it well?"

"Well enough," I said.

"When were you last there?"

"Summer, 1938."

"Six years ago. That's recent enough. It hasn't changed much in that time, except for being occupied by Germans. The buildings and streets remain the same. That'll be your cover story. You're a student teacher from Rouen who's come to stay with relatives in Malerme. That way, if anyone talks to you about Rouen, you'll be able to answer them without getting caught out.

"I'll leave you to work out what you'll need in the way of the right kind of explosives and detonator equipment. That's one of the things you've been trained in, after all." He took a paper file from his desk and handed it to me. "These are for your eyes only, and you can't take them with you when you go, because if you're caught and the Germans find them, they'll identify the target."

I opened the file and took out a small number of photographs. They were of a bridge crossing a river, taken from different angles.

"People died getting these to us," he said. "But we're fairly sure the Germans don't know it's the target."

As I studied the photographs of the bridge, memories of our lectures and practical training in demolition came back to me. Our instructor had been a young man called Ian – although I doubted if that had been his real name.

"Explosives," Ian had told us, gesturing at an array of chemicals laid out on a table in his metal shed. "Are they dangerous to handle? Nitro-glycerine certainly is, it can blow up if it's shaken too much. But most explosives are safe enough until a detonator is brought into the equation. The one we use at SOE is this one, called Explosive 808." He pointed to what looked like six small balls of green plasticine on the table. "Pick it up. Squeeze it in your hand. See what it feels like."

Like the others, I picked up one of the green lumps, but with a certain wariness. I gave the lump a gentle squeeze. It certainly felt like plasticine. As I squeezed it I caught a smell coming from it, like almonds.

"The best sort of detonator to trigger the explosion is electric cable, which means you can get a good distance from the site of the explosion. A length of plastic-covered cable contains two wires, positive and negative. It's just like switching on a light: when negative and positive are connected they complete an electrical circuit, which ignites the charge pushed inside the plastic explosive. Bang."

There had been a lot more, about other ways to set off an explosive charge, and what to do if it didn't go off. All of it, we were told, was dangerous. That had been the theory. Now, I was about to put it into practice. And though part of me was excited about finally going into action, a large part of me felt very sick and very scared.

Chapter 13

Over the next few days everything was prepared for my mission. At the wardrobe department I was measured and fitted out in clothes suitable for a 17-year-old girl in a small village in Normandy. My hair was cut and shaped in the local fashion, and I was given a pair of slightly worn shoes.

"Wear all of these all the time until you go," I was instructed. "The dress, the coat, the shoes, you have to look as if you're used to wearing them."

My own clothes, even my underwear, were confiscated and taken away from me.

"We can't take the chance of you accidentally taking any of your own clothes with you. Labels, the design, anything that suggests English clothes could be your death warrant."

They did, however, give me a thick sheepskin-lined flying jacket and a pair of thick woollen trousers.

"They say you'll be flying over in a Lysander. Trust me, without these you'll freeze to death once you get off the ground. Wear them over your ordinary clothes. These will keep you warm in the plane, but you'll need to dispose of them as soon as you land."

At the Armoury Department I selected the things I'd need to bring the bridge down: plastic explosives, rolls of electric wire, detonator triggers and wire strippers. I was aware that I'd very likely have to carry these things with me to the bridge, so I had to be careful about getting the weight right. Edward Swinton came with me to the Armoury Department to counter-sign for the equipment I selected. Security, as ever, was tight.

"I'll have this lot waiting for you at Tempsford Airfield," he said.

"Where's that?" I asked.

"It's in Bedfordshire," he said. "It's our own special departure point. You'll be taken there by car tomorrow afternoon."

Tomorrow! My mind raced. So soon! Once again, at the thought of actually going, my excitement was mixed with a dreadful feeling of fear. Mr Swinton must have spotted this, because he asked: "That is alright, isn't it?"

"Yes, of course," I said.

"It's alright to be afraid," he said gently. "It's being afraid that helps keep us alive in these situations."

"Were you afraid?" I asked. Then I silently swore at myself for asking the question. He was my boss! And, for all I knew, he'd never actually been on a mission.

But he looked at me sympathetically and nodded.

"All the time," he said. "You never stop feeling scared.

But you just have to remember what you're doing it for. We have to win this war, or the Nazis will rule the world. You can tell your aunt that you're going away on urgent business related to the War."

"Urgent office filing," I laughed.

"Tell her she can always contact me if she doesn't hear from you and gets worried about you," he said. He handed me a small business card. "The number's on there."

"And what will you tell her?" I asked.

"I'll reassure her," he said. "That's what I do. So, at two o'clock tomorrow afternoon a man called Charlie will call and collect you from your aunt's house.

He produced a thick envelope from his briefcase and handed it to me.

"Here is everything you'll need to back up your identity as Céline LeBlanc. French ID card. Birth certificate. Ration book. And all authentic. Well, they look authentic. We have the best people producing them."

"Thank you," I said, taking the envelope. I didn't know whether I ought to go through the documents there in front of him, but I had to trust they knew what they were doing. I would look at them later.

Swinton hesitated, then added: "You do know that if you get into serious trouble, we won't be able to help you. You're on your own."

"Yes," I said.

He held out his hand.

"I wish you good luck," he said.

I shook his hand. "Thank you."

....

That night there was no air raid. Aunt Abbey and I sat in the living room, the blackout curtains pulled shut, the radio on in the background, as she talked about my going off the next day.

"I'm going to miss you, but at least I know you'll be safe," she said. "Well, as safe as anyone can be these days. As it's a government thing, there's bound to be lots of security."

"Yes, I'm sure there will be," I assured her.

"Where is it you're going, Violet?" she asked.

I smiled. "I'm not allowed to say, Aunt Abbey," I said. "Not even to you. I'm sorry."

"But if I need to get in touch with you ..."

"That man whose name is on the card I gave you is the one you can call," I said.

She picked up the card from the sideboard.

"Mr Edward Swinton. Inter-Services Research Bureau."

"That's him," I said.

We listened to the radio a bit longer, a concert of an orchestra playing a selection of popular classical pieces, and then we went to bed.

In my room I opened the envelope Edward Swinton had given me and examined the documents, the proof that I was Céline LeBlanc. Born in Paris. Currently living in Rouen. My photograph stared back at me from the ID card. Everything was stamped with official stamps. There were even a couple of photographs of a little girl who could have been me when I was much younger, with a man and a woman, sitting together on a beach and smiling at the camera. On the back was an inscription in faded ink that said: "Daddy, Mummy and Céline aged 3, Lamor-Plage, Brittany."

I wondered if there really had been a Céline LeBlanc, and what had happened to her. If there had been, I guessed she was no longer alive. I was now Céline LeBlanc.

Chapter 14

The next afternoon a car arrived at our house to take me away. I carried my small suitcase out of the house, then gave Aunt Abbey a really big strong hug. I wanted so much to tell her that I loved her, and how grateful I was for everything she'd done for me, just in case I didn't come back. But I couldn't. I couldn't say anything important, and not being able to say it broke my heart.

"Take care of yourself," she said.

"And you," I replied.

Then I carried my small suitcase to the car and put it in the boot. When we got to Tempsford it would be put into storage to await my return, when I could be Violet Debuchy again. My Céline LeBlanc documents were secure inside my coat.

I looked out of the rear window of the car and saw Aunt Abbey standing on the pavement, waving goodbye, and wondered if I'd ever see her again. Part of me was desperate to go back and stay with her, protect her. But I'd come too far to turn back now.

We drove north out of London and continued going north. Charlie – if that was his name – and I didn't talk much on the journey. For one thing, we couldn't really swap any personal stories or details, and we couldn't talk about where I was going, so we stuck to stuff like the weather, and the radio programmes we'd listened to lately.

After a couple of hours driving, Charlie pulled the car to a halt in a large empty field in a remote part of the Bedfordshire countryside.

"Here we are," he said. "Tempsford."

I looked around me, bewildered. There was nothing here! It was just a farmer's field with a couple of tumbledown derelict buildings, one of which looked like a barn that had been on fire and was now a burnt-out shell, and the other a ruined farmhouse with a collapsed roof that was now just rotten wooden rafters poking up from the half-fallen down walls. On one side of the field were two large piles of hay bales, with a few broken-down tractors and other pieces of farm machinery next to an old, rusty-looking water tank fixed high on some disused scaffolding.

Charlie grinned.

"Clever, isn't it!" he said.

"Clever?" I echoed. "What's clever about it? It's a just an old ruined farm!"

"Yes, that's what it's supposed to look like," he said. "The Germans know there's an airfield here somewhere, but they haven't been able to find it from the air. Or even the ground. We're pretty sure their agents have been searching for it.

"A stage magician created it. It's all a huge illusion. That burnt-out barn, for example. It's done with canvas and paint. Inside, it's a proper control centre with all the best equipment. The same with the old farmhouse. Those rotten timbers are just stage dressing on the top to make it look like the roof's collapsed.

"That water tank, that's the control tower. And look at those piles of hay bales. They disguise two hangars, where the planes are kept. We use Westland Lysanders, which are small two-person planes, so they fit inside nicely."

I sat there in the car looking at the shambles in front of me, astonished. Whoever had created this had done a fantastic job. It looked exactly what it was supposed to look like: a derelict abandoned farm.

Charlie put the car back into gear and drove across the field, pulling up next to the burnt-out barn.

"Here we are," he said.

I followed him to the broken wooden door, which looked as if it was hanging off one hinge, and was surprised to see when I got up close that this was yet another illusion of clever painting and carpentry. We went into the barn and found ourselves in a small aircraft hangar. A small plane was inside, and a man wearing a thick leather jacket and a flying helmet looked like he was tinkering with the engine.

"Your passenger's here, Jim!" said Charlie.

Jim stepped away from the plane, ducking under the

wing, and came towards us, smiling in welcome.

"Welcome to Fantasy Farm!" he greeted me. He gestured towards the plane. "Just making sure that everything's in order for the flight. You know the drill?"

"We'll be flying at night with no lights," I said. "You land in a field and I jump out."

"That's about it," nodded Jim. "Hopefully the Germans won't spot us and shoot at us. The Lysander is a great little flier, but it's not built for attack by bullets and rockets. They'll go straight through the outer skin."

As his words sank in, I felt sick. That was one thing that hadn't occurred to me, bullets going through the outer skin of the plane and killing us.

I looked at the plane which was painted completely black in the hope it wouldn't be spotted easily at night. I just hoped it worked.

There were two small cockpits, with a ladder leading up to the rear one.

"That's where you go," said Jim. "The ladder's so you can get down without having to jump too far. We don't want you damaging yourself."

"I've done parachute training," I pointed out.

"That may be, but you'd be surprised how many people sprain an ankle jumping just a little distance." He looked at his watch. "We'll be heading off as soon as it gets dark, in about an hour."

"Fine," I said.

"You know that if there are no fires to guide us in, we'll have to abandon and come back," he said. "It'll mean the Germans are wise to the game. If that's the case, they might well know we're coming in, so there could be shooting. But hopefully everything will be alright." And he gave me a grin, but there was something false about it.

"What's the matter?" I asked.

He looked at me, startled.

"Why should anything be the matter?"

"I've been trained to spot when people are covering up something," I said.

Jim hesitated, then gave an unhappy sigh.

"Okay," he said. "If you must know, something's been hanging over me for a couple of days. Something a bit upsetting. But I'll get over it. We all do."

"What?" I asked.

Again, he hesitated, then he looked around to make sure we weren't overheard before saying. "If I tell you, you're not to tell anyone else I told you."

"I promise," I said.

"I just feel I need to talk to someone, but we're not allowed to talk about things like this in case it lowers morale."

"What happened?"

"Guy. He was my ... my best friend," said Jim. "Three

days ago he took off with one of your crowd. A girl. Someone must have betrayed them, or maybe it was an accident. Anyway, as he came into land, his plane got shot up. It caught fire." He fell silent, and I saw his hand go to his face to wipe away a tear. "They both died."

"I'm sorry," I said.

"I needed to say it to someone, but there's no one here I can talk to. And I can't talk to anyone outside about what we do." He wiped his eyes again, then took a deep breath. "Please, don't tell anyone I told you."

"I won't," I assured him. "Who was the girl?"

"The girl?"

"The one Guy was taking."

"Her name was Yvette."

Chapter 15

I was too stunned to respond. Jim talked for a bit longer about his friend Guy, but I wasn't listening. Yvette, dead. Although she hadn't been part of my group, in a way she had been the one person I felt close to. Maybe it had been the friendly way she'd come up to me when we were at the army base and told me how glad she was I'd got through the "gossip and questioning" test. Whatever it was, I'd liked her. And now she was gone.

Had she been scared, I wondered. Mr Swinton had said that everyone felt scared. That the fear kept us on edge, kept us alive. But nothing could save you if your plane was shot down and burst into flames.

I did my best to force the image out of my mind. I looked at Jim and saw how desperately miserable he looked. Once we were up there, the same thing could happen to us.

"I'm sorry," I apologized to Jim. "I do feel for you."

Jim looked as if he was fighting back his tears. He gestured at the open doors of the hangar.

"It's nearly time," he said. "The moon is up. You'd better check you've got everything."

I nodded and went to a bench where there were two bags labelled with the name 'Céline'. I opened them and checked the contents. Everything was there: plastic explosive, coils of wire, detonators, wire strippers.

"Everything's there," I said, closing the bags.

"Okay," said Jim.

He signalled to two mechanics and they rolled the plane out of the hangar into the open air. I climbed up the ladder, settled myself in the rear seat and strapped myself in. Jim hauled the two bags of plastic explosives and wires up the ladder and handed them to me. I dumped them on my lap. There was nowhere else in the tiny cockpit to put them. Jim climbed into the cockpit in front of me and pulled his hatch down. I did the same, fixing mine into place with the catches.

"Testing intercom," Jim's voice came over the tiny speaker by my side. "One two three. Do you read?"

I clicked the button on the handset.

"Reading you loud and clear," I said.

"Roger," said Jim.

There were the sounds of ignition up front and around me, followed by a roar as the propeller sprang to life, starting slowly at first, then getting faster and faster until it was barely visible as a shimmering blur in the darkness.

There was another click, then Jim's voice said: "Okay. We're ready to roll."

The sound of the plane's engine built up, getting higher

and higher. Suddenly Jim engaged the drive gear and the plane began to roll forward, gaining speed quickly, rushing across the open field. Even though I guessed Jim had done this many times before, I marvelled at how he could see to aim the plane in this darkness. The plane bumped and lurched a couple of times, and the next second we were lifting up.

As we rose higher, it got colder, and I was glad I'd put on thick socks and was wearing the heavy woollen trousers over my skirt, as well as the thick leather flying jacket over my blouse and light jacket. As we flew I couldn't get the thought of Yvette and her plane being shot down out of my mind. I looked at the bags of explosives on my lap. There was enough here to bring down a railway bridge. If we were shot at, the bullets would pass straight through the plane's thin skin, hit the explosives, and we would be blown to bits. I did my best to push that thought out of my mind, but it wasn't easy.

We flew on for what seemed like hours, flying low. Jim and I didn't talk over the radio – the engine was too loud to make communication easy, and Jim needed to concentrate. We were flying without lights over a country that was mostly dark because, like us in England, the Germans were sticking to blackout rules in France as a protection against bombing air raids.

"There it is!" came Jim's voice over the radio.

I looked down, and saw four small fires in the distance,

creating a box shape. My heart leapt. This was it!

"Let's hope the Germans haven't spotted it!" he said.

Or perhaps they've set up a fake landing and are lying in wait for us, I thought nervously.

The plane began to fly lower, and soon we were barely above tree height, getting lower and lower, and all the time I was tense, expecting to hear the sound of machine guns opening up.

Then there was a bump, and the small plane bounced, leaping up into the air, before coming down again, shuddering and shaking as Jim put on the brakes.

"Go!" he said.

I undid the catch fastening the hatch cover, then threw out the two bags. I followed them immediately, dropping down from the rear cockpit, not bothering to use the ladder, and landed with a thud on the earth. I put my parachute training into use, rolling with the fall and springing to my feet.

I saw two dark shapes scoop up my two bags and run with them, as a voice close to me said urgently in French: "This way!"

A large bulky middle-aged man and a tall thin young man each grabbed me by an arm and hustled me towards the hedge that bordered the field, following the two who had my bags. Behind us, others were hard at work throwing earth into the four holes in the ground, putting out the signal fires. The plane's engine hadn't stopped, and now I heard it rev into life again with a throaty sound, and then turn and accelerate.

The ground beneath my feet was uneven and rutted, causing me to nearly fall a few times, and I realized: this is why they're holding me. They don't want me falling over and spraining an ankle or something.

We reached the hedge, and ran alongside it until we came to a gate. On the other side of the gate was an old battered van. The rear doors were open and my bags were being thrown in.

"In!" snapped the middle-aged man.

He got behind the steering wheel, while the younger man helped me inside the back of the van. Then he climbed in and pulled the doors shut.

The van jerked forward, the sudden jolt sending me sprawling, but my fall was cushioned by a pile of sacks, sending a cloud of powder to rise from them, making me cough.

"Flour," explained the young man. "We're in the baker's van, Jules Lemaître. I'm Pierre Megris."

"I don't think you're supposed to tell me your real names, in case I get caught," I told him.

The young man laughed.

"As you're staying with my family at our home, that won't work," he said. "And Monsieur Lemaître is the one you'll need to go and see if you're in trouble. So you have to know who he is. The others …" he shrugged. "You're right, you don't need to know their names. But I'm sure you'll work out who they are once we start work." He handed me an empty sack. "Put your flying jacket and things in there. That way, if we get stopped, we can try and persuade them you're along to help load the flour. But it won't work if you're dressed up looking like you've just got off a plane."

I did as Pierre said, taking off my jacket and putting it in the sack, along with the things I'd brought with me. Pierre pushed the sack beneath the pile of others, hiding it along with my two bags. So far, I was impressed by their organization. But then, if they hadn't been so organized they wouldn't have stayed alive this long.

"You'll be staying with me and my mother and my little sister, Mimi," continued Pierre.

"And your father?" I asked, and as I said it I wished I'd kept my mouth shut. From the angry expression on Pierre's face I knew I'd touched a raw nerve.

"My father's dead," said Pierre bitterly. "He was killed in the War."

I was on the point of saying "So was mine", but stopped myself in time, remembering the instruction: never give information about yourself, even to someone you think is a friend.

"I'm sorry," I apologized. "That was thoughtless of me."

He shook his head.

"His death will be avenged," he said. "That is why you

are here." He shrugged, as if dismissing the subject, and said: "When we get home we'll get your clothes dusted down and lose that flour from them."

"Did you have to come and pick me up in a van filled with sacks of flour?" I asked.

Pierre grinned.

"Of course," he said. "Like I said, Jules is a baker, and if he's ever stopped by a patrol he's got the perfect excuse for being out at night: he's getting flour for the early morning baking. No flour, no bread." He laughed. "The Germans think he's okay, because he gives their soldiers cakes and pastries when they come into his bakery. What they don't realize is that he lets them talk and gossip, and listens to what's going on, and reports it back."

"He's a brave man."

"He is," said Pierre. "And he's not the only one. There are plenty around here who take chances to defeat the Germans."

"Like you," I said.

Even in the darkness inside the van, I could see I'd embarrassed him. Mentally, I kicked myself. Despite all my intentions to remain cool and calm, I was talking too much. I guessed it was the excitement of actually being on a mission, being here, in France, behind enemy lines, and meeting the Resistance. I decided to keep my mouth shut; at least, until we were safely indoors.

Chapter 16

The van dropped us off at a cottage at the outskirts of a village. Pierre and I hauled the two bags and the sack containing my flying jacket out of the van, slammed the doors shut, and it drove off.

The front door of the cottage opened and two figures hurried out, an older woman and a girl of about ten. They helped us carry the stuff inside and, once the front door was shut and locked and bolted, they ushered Pierre and me into a small kitchen, where an oil lamp threw out an eerie yellow glow.

"Welcome!" said the woman, and she gave me a broad smile and a hug.

"Maman, this is Céline LeBlanc," introduced Pierre. "Céline, this is my mother."

"Madam Megris," I said, returning her hug.

"No no," she rebuked me. "You are supposed to be the daughter of an old friend of mine, and if that was the case you would call me Aunt Berthe."

"Aunt Berthe," I nodded.

"And this is Mimi," said Pierre.

I looked down at a little girl and marvelled at how children as young as this were also putting their lives on the line for the cause.

"Hello," said the girl. "Thank you for coming here."

"Thank you for letting me stay with you," I replied.

"You must be cold and tired after your journey, and you will want to be about your business tomorrow," said Berthe. "So let's put some hot food inside you and get you to bed. You'll be sharing with Mimi."

"You have my bed. I've made up a mattress on the floor for me," said Mimi.

"Absolutely not!" I said. "It's good enough of you to let me share your room. I'm certainly not going to put you out of your bed!"

"But you are special!" insisted Mimi. "You are a warrior!"

"And warriors don't need a bed to sleep in," I said. "A mattress is more than comfortable."

The first thing we did was to take my bags, with the explosives and detonators, and hide them in the attic. After that, Berthe put some steaming hot onion soup into two bowls for Pierre and me. It was delicious! Once again it made me realize the different qualities of food available in cities and rural areas, and I determined that when this war was over, I would do my best to try and make a life for myself in the countryside.

Although I was tired and should have slept, the

excitement of the journey here to France, and thoughts of what lay ahead, kept me awake. When I finally fell asleep, it seemed I'd only had my eyes closed for a short while before Mimi was gently shaking me.

"Good morning," she said. "Maman has bread and coffee ready for you for breakfast."

The bread was delicious, fresh out of the oven. The coffee, though, had a peculiar taste.

"It's made from acorns and dandelion roots," explained Berthe, seeing my puzzled expression as I sipped at it. "We haven't had proper coffee here for a long while, and what there is, the Germans take."

"Where is Pierre?" I asked.

"He has gone to work. He works at Brubel's hardware shop. We shall call in there later. It will be a good thing to take you round the village to meet people, to let them see who you are, and that you are one of ours. That will stop them asking questions about you. You are one of us. Céline LeBlanc, the daughter of an old friend of mine from Rouen."

"Come to stay with you following the unfortunate death of my mother," I added. "She died recently from pneumonia. It's still too painful for me to talk about."

"Good," nodded Berthe. "Keep to that and it will stop them asking too many questions. From you, that is. They will ask me, of course, and I will tell them the same. What were you doing in Rouen?"

"I'm training to be a teacher," I said.

"Good," nodded Berthe again. "Nothing too complicated."

After breakfast, I set off with Berthe and Mimi to be introduced around the village. Their cottage was at the end of the village, which meant a short walk, but it was very pleasant for me. It brought back memories of when I was small and Mum and Dad used to take me out into the country, to villages very much like this one, Malerme.

As we neared the main square in the village, where the church and school and the different shops were clustered, I saw the first signs of the German occupation. Almost every corner seemed to have a machine gun post, with soldiers guarding the machine gun behind piles of sandbags.

"Do they need that much protection?" I whispered to Berthe.

"They think they do," Berthe whispered back. "They are terrified of the Resistance launching an attack. But here in Malerme, the boys have decided to play it safe. They concentrate on disrupting German lines of communication. Cutting telephone lines, that sort of thing. Annoying to the Germans, but not fatal. The last thing we want are more and more Germans coming into the village, especially with what you plan to do."

She suddenly stopped talking and smiled and nodded at a middle-aged woman walking towards them, who nodded in return, although she didn't smile. The woman walked on, but I could feel her eyes watching me behind our backs.

"Madame Poitiers," whispered Berthe. "A dangerous woman. She sneaks information to the Germans."

"Why?" I asked, surprised.

"To get in favour with them," said Berthe. "Unfortunately, there are a few people like that in the village. A few do it because, believe it or not, they are Nazis and actually support Hitler. Some do it out of fear, because they are afraid of the Germans and hope the Germans will leave them alone if they co-operate. In some parts of France, the Resistance killed German soldiers. The Germans retaliated by killing ten French people for every soldier who was killed, and fifty people for every officer who was attacked." She sighed bitterly. "That sort of thing makes people very frightened for the safety of them and their family. So they collaborate with the Germans, passing on information about who might be in the Resistance, and gossip about people who've been heard saying bad things about Germans.

"We know most of the people who do it, so we're careful what we say when we're around them. But there might be others who are kind to your face, but we don't know what they're saying behind your back. So the rule is: trust no one."

Exactly the same words that Mr Swinton had drummed into me.

Our first port of call was Brubel's hardware shop, where

Pierre was behind the counter. I was introduced to the owner, and his wife who came from the back of the shop to shake hands and welcome me, their expressions very sympathetic to me. From there, we moved on to the bakery, where I was introduced by Berthe to the bulky middle-aged man who'd hustled me into his van the night before.

"Monsieur Lemaître, this is Céline. She's from Rouen. She will be staying with us for a while."

The baker gave me a welcoming smile.

"Good morning, Mam'selle," he said. "Welcome to our village. You will find life different here after Rouen. Less rushing around. A better quality of life, in my opinion."

"I am sure I will like it here," I replied. "Aunt Berthe has been very welcoming."

From the bakery we moved on to a newsagents, then a greengrocer's, and at every shop I was introduced to the owners and the other customers by Madame Megris with handshakes and smiles of welcome. My identity and back-story was being firmly established.

I soon caught the mood of the village – who was anti-German, and who seemed to support them. The most prominent of the German supporters we met was the village mayor, a small, pompous man in his sixties with a pencil-thin moustache and a superior air. We came face to face with him on the street as we walked out of the haberdashers.

"M'sieur le Maire," said Madame Megris respectfully.

"Permit me to introduce an old friend of our family, Miss Céline LeBlanc from Rouen. She is staying with us for a while following …" She hesitated, the lowered her voice as she added: "a family tragedy."

"My condolences, Mam'selle," said the Mayor, though there was little in his tone of voice to suggest real sympathy. His manner was brusque and self-important. "Are you a patriot?"

The question took me by surprise for a moment. Then I nodded.

"Yes," I assured him. "I am."

"You wish France to survive and prosper?"

"Of course," I said.

"I understand that in Rouen the criminals of the Resistance have been murdering good people who would make France strong," he said, his tone challenging as he looked at me questioningly, searching for my reaction.

"The criminals of the Resistance will not win," I said.

He nodded, my answer satisfying him.

"I am glad to hear you say that, Mam'selle," he said.

With that, he nodded at Madame Megris, and walked on.

"What a horrible little man," I whispered.

"You did well," Madame Megris whispered back. "He is dangerous. And protected by the Germans."

Chapter 17

That evening, after our meal, Pierre and I finally got the chance to talk about my mission: the destruction of the railway bridge over the River Clemel.

"The British want the bridge blown up by the fourth of June," I told him.

"Why?" asked Pierre. "Is something big happening then?"

I shrugged and shook my head.

"I don't know," I replied. "Even if there was, they wouldn't tell me."

Pierre looked suddenly angry and desperate at the same time. "Five years this has been going on!" he burst out. "Five years living under Nazi control! Sometimes I think I will just get a gun and go out and shoot them all myself! This cannot go on!"

"It will end," I assured him. "The British and the Americans are doing all they can to free France."

"But it is taking so long! You can't know what it has been like for us here!"

For all of us, I thought. I wanted to say to him: my parents are dead, too, Pierre – killed in this war. My father died here in France. But I said nothing.

"The fourth of June," said Pierre. "The day after tomorrow."

I nodded.

"We'll do it tomorrow night," I said. "I need to go out and see it this evening, to check things out."

Pierre nodded.

"We'll take the bikes. You ride Mimi's. We'll make a visit to my Aunt Marie, taking her some bread and other provisions from my mother. The road to her house goes near the bridge."

And so later that day Pierre and I set off on the bikes, the baskets at the front loaded with a loaf of bread and tubs of jam and chutney. On our way we passed a German patrol car heading towards the village, but they didn't stop us: we were just two young people running an errand on our bikes.

The railway bridge was about two miles outside the village. We stopped and pulled the bikes off the road and sat on the edge of a wooden fence. To anyone watching, we were just taking a break from our cycle ride.

A patch of wasteland, filled with weeds, was between the road and the single railway track. This wasteland continued on the other side of the railway track and ended at a small, dark wood, which then dipped down and disappeared.

"The wood goes down to the river," explained Pierre. "Do you want to get nearer to the bridge?"

I shook my head.

"If anyone sees us going to it, it might arouse suspicion. I just needed to see the real location. I've got a good idea of the actual bridge from the photos we were sent."

Pierre nodded.

"M'sieur Lemaître's son, Andre, took them," he said. "He's good with a camera." He smiled. "He pretended to be taking photographs of birds and animals on the river."

"I guess he took some of those as well."

"Of course." He looked towards the railway bridge, a hundred yards away across the patch of wasteland. "How many people will you need?"

"Three," I said. "You, me and one other to keep watch."

"Are you sure that's enough?"

"The more people who are involved, the more chance there is of word leaking out," I reminded him. "I'll fix the explosives to the bridge. You run the detonator cables from the bridge to our hiding place. The other person will keep a look-out and signal if anyone's coming."

"What about transport?" asked Pierre. "Monsieur Lemaître's van?"

"These bicycles," I told him. "Easier to hide than a car. We can carry the equipment in the baskets."

"Tomorrow night, then."

"Tomorrow night."

The next day was strange. On one level it seemed to rush by at the realization that, at last, I was going to be blowing up a bridge behind enemy lines, and for real, not just a practice, with Germans everywhere. At the same time, the day seemed to drag, the minutes going by so slowly. I was eager to get into action, but at the same time I was nervous. I'd seen from my training that so many things could go wrong. The detonators could fail. The cable connections could fail. We might be spotted by a passing patrol. The thought of all the things that could go wrong terrified me, and I had to work hard to try and keep myself calm, taking lots of deep breaths and telling myself that all my hard training would see me through and make this operation succeed.

I did my best to try and appear normal, going with Berthe to the village for supplies. Taking Mimi to school. Forcing myself to take part in pleasant conversations with people we met. And all the time running through the mission in my head: planting the right amount of explosives in the correct areas, setting off the detonators.

We had to wait until after midnight before it was dark enough for us to go on our mission. A man in his thirties, who Pierre called Martin, arrived at about ten that night. He spent most of the time in the house sitting in the kitchen and regarding me suspiciously, as if he was doubtful that a girl like me could carry out this sort of work. I recognized that look, because when the others girls and I had been training, I'd seen that same expression on the faces of some of the male soldiers we'd met, who obviously viewed us with suspicion.

I went out of the back door to watch the sky and listen to the sounds of the night, alert for the sound of vehicles on the road. Everything in the immediate area seemed quiet.

"Okay," I said. "Let's go."

Martin, Pierre and I hauled the bags down from the attic, and then loaded them onto two of the bikes which had baskets on the front: Pierre's and Mimi's. Martin had his own bike, and the three of us set off. The road was quiet and empty, and with enough of a moon for us to be able to see as we rode. About half a mile before we reached the bridge, Pierre pulled his bicycle to a halt and gestured at a gap in a fence by the side of the road.

"This way," he said.

We pushed our bikes through the gap, then rode across the bumpy wasteland towards a small wood that went down to the River Clemel. Once we reached the wood, we pushed the bikes into hiding in the trees.

"Whistle if you hear anything," Pierre muttered to Martin, who nodded.

Pierre took one bag, I the other, and we made our way towards the bridge, keeping just inside the wood. I could see the moonlight glinting on the metal of the railway lines that ran across the area of wasteland.

"Where do you want these wires?" asked Pierre, taking the reels of wire out of the bag.

"Leave the ends hooked over that branch," I said, pointing to a small tree close to the bridge. "Make sure there's enough wire for me to run them to the middle of the bridge. Then take the other ends back as far as you can. And make sure the two wires don't touch."

Pierre slipped back into the trees, while I carried the bag with the plastic explosives and detonators to the bridge. I was just about to open the bag and start taking out the explosives, when I heard an owl hoot. It was almost the sound of an owl, but not quite. Martin was signalling a warning.

I grabbed the bag and rushed to the cover of the trees in a crouching run, getting there just in time as lights cut through the darkness and I heard the sound of a car engine. A vehicle was bouncing across the wasteland, its headlights half-covered at the top to stop them shining too brightly.

The vehicle pulled to a halt some distance away, close to the railway line. I peered out from behind the cover of the trees and bushes, my heart thumping as I saw the doors open and two soldiers get out, both carrying rifles.

What had happened? Had the Germans got word of what I was planning? But the only person I'd told about my mission was Pierre, and the only person he'd told was

Martin. Had Martin betrayed us? No, because he'd just given the signal to warn us.

I racked my brains for how the Germans might have discovered what my mission was; but unless there had been a leak from inside London HQ, I couldn't think how. The Resistance hadn't been alerted beforehand to the target of my mission, just that I would be arriving.

I cursed myself for not bringing a pistol with me. I'd been told I wouldn't need one for this mission, but if I'd gone with my instincts and brought one, I could silence these two Germans and go ahead with blowing up the bridge.

I ducked behind a tree as the Germans clicked on torches and walked beside the railway line towards the bridge, following their beams of light, all the time getting closer to my position. Nearer and nearer they came and then, as they reached the bridge, they stopped. They moved forward, and I heard their boots clattering on the wood and metal. The lights from their torches shone along the rails, and from side to side of the bridge. Then one of them said something brief in German, with the other giving a grunt that sounded like agreement, and they turned and walked back beside the railway line to their vehicle.

The torches went out, the doors opened and shut, the vehicle started up and they drove away.

I let out a long sigh of relief. Just a routine inspection, then.

I waited until the red tail lights had disappeared, then I grabbed the bag and hurried back to the bridge. I slid down the earthy slope until I got to the support nearest to this side of the river. The support was old, made of stone. This bridge had been there for years. It looked as if an old road bridge had been added to to make it wide and strong enough to take railway trains. I moved beneath the bridge, running my hands over the place where the stone support met the timbers of the bridge, searching for what's known as 'the keystone'. It's the core of the construction in most buildings, most bridges, the focal point of the pressure. The aim of demolition is to find this focal point and blow it, and let the rest of the construction collapse under its own weight.

I found the keystone and pushed the plastic into the crevices and around it.

When I was satisfied that was done properly, I carried the bag up to the bridge itself, and walked along the railway lines until I was at the centre. I forced the plastic in between the cracks of the old timbers, then packed more on either side of the metal railway lines.

When all the plastic was in place, I pushed the detonators into the plastic.

My last action was to collect the ends of the wire Pierre had left dangling over the branch and carry it to the different detonators, then strip the plastic covering off the wire and connect the ends to the detonators.

I scooped up the empty bag and hurried back through the wood, watching out for Pierre and Martin. I saw them waiting for me. Pierre was sitting on the ground, guarding the end of the reel of cable and holding the ends of the wires firmly apart.

"Right, let's do it," I said.

I took the ends of the cables from him.

"What happens if it doesn't work?" he asked.

I weighed up his question.

"If it doesn't, I go back to see why not," I told him. "It should be alright, but sometimes a connection can come loose."

"And if it clicks back in place when you're there?" asked Martin.

I forced a grin I didn't really feel.

"In that case, I'll have done my bit for the war effort." I looked at them. "You two might as well get off. I can do this."

"We're staying with you," said Pierre firmly.

"Okay," I said.

I stripped the ends of the two cables, then pushed the bare ends into opposite ends of a metal tube.

"Here we go," I said.

I pressed a switch, completing the circuit.

There was a brief pause, and then a huge WWHOOOOMPPPPFFFF! from the bridge, followed by another, and then another. The sky lit up orange and yellow, and then the acrid smell of burning came to us, followed by the sound of a massive rumble, the earth around us shaking.

"It's going!" said Pierre excitedly. "The bridge is going!"

From this distance, and in the darkness, even with the moon, it was hard to see, but there was no doubt that parts of the bridge had collapsed. How much? I wondered. Had enough of it collapsed to make it impossible to repair?

"Time to go," I said. "They'll have heard that in the village. The Germans will be along any minute."

"What about the cables?" asked Pierre, pointing at the electric wires.

"Leave them," I said. "No time to grab things up. Let's go!"

We grabbed up our bikes.

"We stay off-road," said Pierre. "Otherwise we'll run into the Germans. I know a way across country. It's rough, but safer." He turned to Martin. "The Corpse Road."

"Good," nodded Martin.

I followed them on Mimi's bike as we rode over the wasteland, and then took a detour into woods, over bumpy tracks, carrying the bikes over fallen trees, through swampy ground. In the distance we could hear the sounds of sirens and vehicles, see lights on the road through the trees.

Finally, after a series of detours, we made it to the back garden of Pierre's house. Martin carried on, while Pierre and I headed indoors, muddy, tired, but exhilarated. We'd done it!

Chapter 18

Before we went to bed, we cleaned the mud off the bikes, just in case the Germans spotted the tracks and came round the village inspecting bikes. We threw some dry earth and dust on them, so they didn't look too clean.

Next morning, we were up early for breakfast. Neither Berthe nor Mimi asked us what we had been up to while we were out, and we didn't offer any information to them. Everyone knew the rules: say nothing.

Pierre was just putting on his coat to go to work, when there was a banging on the front door. Immediately, we all shot worried looks at one another. Was it the Germans?

Berthe opened the door, and we breathed a little as we saw it was the next-door neighbour, Madame Peroux. She was in a terrible state, panicking.

"Madame Megris! Something terrible has happened!"

"Oh?"

"Someone has blown up the Clemel bridge!"

Berthe stared at her, open-mouthed, shocked. Berthe was a good actress, but the news might well have shocked her.

"Are you sure?" she gasped.

Madame Peroux nodded, fear showing clearly on her face.

"It's completely destroyed! The Germans are furious! They are going through the village, questioning everybody. Some say it's the Resistance, but others say it's the Maquis." She shook her head, then asked beseechingly. "What are we to do?"

"Nothing," said Berthe firmly. "This is nothing to do with us."

"But we will suffer!" said Madame Peroux, and she began to cry.

"It will be alright," Berthe tried to calm her down. "You won't be in any trouble. Come in and sit down."

And Berthe brought Madame Peroux into the kitchen, where Mimi was getting her things ready for school.

"Leave that," Berthe told Mimi. "Things are going to be bad in the village today. You'd better stay home. I'll write a note saying you're not well."

"But Elise and I are making an island!" protested Mimi.

"You can do it tomorrow," said Berthe.

"I'll call in at the school on my way to work and tell them," said Pierre. "I'll say it's a cold."

"You'd better be careful today," Berthe warned him.

"I will," he promised her.

After he'd gone, I shot a glance at Madame Peroux, sitting at the kitchen table, twisting a handkerchief nervously between her hands, and whispered to Berthe: "I'm going into the village to see what the Germans are up to."

"It's too dangerous," said Berthe,

"I have to. I need to report back."

"They will suspect you. You are a stranger."

"They will be looking for men, not a girl," I told her.

"They will be suspecting everyone," said Berthe.

"I will be fine," I said, but I could see doubt in her face. "You'd better get back to Madame Peroux."

I put on my coat and walked towards the centre of the village. It was a very different atmosphere from the day before: armoured cars were parked in the village square, armed soldiers were everywhere, stopping people and ordering them to open their bags and turn out their pockets. They were searching everyone: men, women, children, all ages. I was stopped and my papers inspected and my pockets searched. The soldiers who stopped me were nervous, frightened. Yesterday, these soldiers had been relaxed, confident, striding about as if they owned the village – which they did. Today, they were desperately trying to hide their feelings of panic, on edge for another attack, another explosion, one that could wipe them out.

I was stopped and searched twice before I reached the village square. It was noticeable that there were fewer villagers out today. I guessed many of them had decided to do the same as Berthe, stay at home, and keep their children at home.

As I was passing Brubel's hardware store, I heard angry voices from inside, and recognized one of them as Pierre's. Alert to the fact that this could signal a problem, I went into the shop. Pierre was engaged in an angry exchange with the small figure of the Mayor. Monsieur Brubel hovered anxiously, making frantic gestures to Pierre to calm down and shut up, while the other customers in the shop watched the argument warily.

"It doesn't matter whether it was the Resistance who blew up the bridge, or just some lone wolf. Whoever did it has put everyone in this village in danger!" shouted the Mayor.

"The people in this village were already in danger!" retorted Pierre just as loudly, and angrily.

"From the Germans?" challenged the Mayor, glaring at Pierre angrily.

I was relieved to see that Pierre shut his mouth and said nothing.

"Let me tell you, young man, I'm glad the Germans are here! They are keeping us safe!" the Mayor ranted.

"Who from?" demanded Pierre, stung.

"From communists!"

"You'd rather have Germans running this country than French people?" shouted Pierre, and I could see that he was getting angrier and angrier.

"Pierre …" I murmured warningly.

Neither Pierre nor the angry Mayor appeared to hear me, they were so wrapped up in their furious argument.

"Yes!" shouted the Mayor. "Because all French Communists will do is hand this country over to their masters in Russia! They are traitors to France!"

"As are those who side with the Germans!" raged Pierre.

"Like me, you mean!" growled the Mayor.

"Yes!" spat Pierre.

At this, there were worried murmurs among those in the shop.

The Mayor glared at Pierre, breathing heavily, and then suddenly he swung his right hand hard, slapping Pierre across the face.

"You dare to call me a traitor!" he roared. "I fought for this country in the last war!"

"And now you sell it to the Germans!" shouted Pierre, and then, before anyone could stop him, he lashed out, his fist catching the Mayor full in the face.

The Mayor stumbled back, and then tumbled backwards and fell on the floor. Blood was pouring down from his nose.

"Leave!" M'sieur Brubel suddenly shouted at Pierre, pointing at the door.

"But …," protested Pierre.

"Leave! Now!" repeated Brubel.

I grabbed hold of Pierre by the arm.

"We must go," I told him urgently.

Chapter 19

Pierre snatched his jacket from me and stormed out of the shop, furious, heading homewards. I hurried after him.

"That was stupid!" I raged at him.

"The Mayor has been deserving that for a long time!" snapped Pierre.

"You can't afford to upset him!" I insisted. "He's a powerful man!"

"Yet he fell on his backside!" retorted Pierre, and he gave a harsh laugh.

Because of the speed Pierre was going at, we arrived home very quickly. Fortunately, Madame Peroux had gone back to her house. One look at the expressions on our faces told Berthe that something was wrong.

"Pierre punched the Mayor," I told her. "He accused the Mayor of being a traitor to France. He spoke out against the Germans."

"And not before time!" spat Pierre. "I've been keeping silent too long. We all have!"

Berthe looked at him, aghast, and shook her head despairingly.

"You know the Germans will have to take action against you! You'd better leave. Go and stay with Uncle Albert and Aunt Jeanne for a while."

"I'm not being driven out of my home by the Germans!" stormed Pierre angrily.

"You have to," insisted Berthe. "If you stay here and the Germans come for you, they'll come for Céline as well."

"Why?" demanded Pierre.

"Because if you are suspect, then so is she! And she is a stranger here!"

"Your mother's right, Pierre," I said.

"But who will help you?" he asked me.

"The others," I said.

"No," said Berthe. "You will have to go as well, Céline. They will take you in just because you are here with us. They may not suspect you at the moment, but once they start questioning you …"

"I won't say anything!" I assured them.

"That's what everyone says," sighed Berthe. She shook her head. "But once the questioning starts …"

The sound of cars pulling up outside the cottage made us all stop talking. Mimi looked out and said with a shock, "It's the Gestapo!"

"So soon!" exclaimed Pierre, alarmed.

"Of course! It is the Mayor! They have to make an example of you," snapped Berthe. "Quick, Pierre! Céline!

Up to the attic!"

"No," said Pierre. "They know I'm here. If they don't find me, they'll take you and Mimi in, Maman. Take Céline up there and hide her."

"But …" I began.

"No time!" Berthe shouted, and she grabbed me by the arm and hustled me towards the stairs.

"I'll be alright," Pierre promised me.

Then Berthe was pushing me up the stairs.

"I've got documents!" I protested. "I can persuade them I'm just an innocent person."

"You don't know the Gestapo!" retorted Berthe.

Oh yes I do, I thought grimly. They killed my father.

Under Berthe's urgings, I climbed up the short wooden ladder into the attic. Berthe pulled the ladder away and started to carry it downstairs. Her last words were: "Shut the trapdoor and don't make a sound, whatever happens!"

I lowered the trapdoor and slid the bolt to keep it shut. I made my way across the bare boards to the inside of the sloping roof. There was a crack in two of the tiles, allowing me to peer out.

There were three cars outside. The doors of the cars were open and a man wearing the black leather coat worn by the Gestapo stood by the first car while armed soldiers approached the cottage. Other soldiers waited by the other two cars, their guns pointed at the cottage, ready to fire.

I heard a banging at the front door and a shout in German ordering them to open up. I heard the door open, and then Pierre's voice demanding to know what was happening. There was the thud of a rifle butt and I heard Pierre cry out in pain.

My first instinct was to throw open the trapdoor and rush downstairs to go to the family's defence, but I restrained myself. That would do no good. In fact, my presence as a suspicious person would harm the family.

Through the crack in the tiles I saw Berthe and Mimi walking out of the house. Then came Pierre, being half-dragged by two German soldiers. The Gestapo officer gestured towards the second car, and the soldiers pushed Mimi and Berthe into the back seats.

The soldiers holding Pierre brought him to stand in front of the Gestapo officer, who began barking questions at him. Meanwhile other soldiers were searching the cottage, their heavy boots crashing as they went from room to room downstairs, opening cupboards. I heard their feet on the wooden stairs, and the sounds as they went into the bedrooms, ripping the sheets and blankets from the beds, opening and closing cupboards.

Please don't let them come up here into the attic, I prayed silently.

I kicked myself mentally for not having brought a revolver with me.

Outside, the Gestapo officer was still firing questions angrily at Pierre, but Pierre remained silent, just glaring defiantly at the officer. Frustrated, the officer suddenly hit out at Pierre, the back of his hand striking Pierre across the face. Pierre stumbled back, then checked himself and regained his balance. Before anyone knew what was happening, Pierre had lashed out at the Gestapo officer, his clenched fist punching the officer full in the face. The officer staggered back and crashed into the side of the car, as the two soldiers leapt on Pierre and gripped him by the arms.

Blood was coming from the Gestapo officer's nose. The officer straightened up, a snarl on his face, and then he pulled his revolver from its holster, pointed it at Pierre, and pulled the trigger.

No!

There was a shriek of anguish from the other car and Berthe tried to get out, but she was pushed back into the car by two soldiers and the door was slammed shut.

I had to stuff my fist into my mouth to stop myself from crying out.

No! Not Pierre!

The sound of the gunshot outside had brought the soldiers searching the house to a stop, and I heard their boots clattering down the stairs, and then saw them hurry out of the cottage.

The Gestapo officer pointed at Pierre and rapped out a

Chapter 20

I weighed up my options. I needed to get to M'sieur Lemaître for help.

With Pierre dead and Berthe and Mimi arrested, the Germans would be watching out for me, because Berthe had done such a good job of introducing me around the village as one of 'their own'.

I thought of trying to disguise myself, as we'd been trained to do, but although a disguise might have worked in a large city with lots of people, it wouldn't in a small village like Malerme where everybody knew everyone else. The only time I could take a chance and go into the village would be at nightfall. But that was many hours away, and it was quite possible that – under interrogation – Berthe or Mimi might be forced into revealing my hiding place in the attic.

So, I couldn't go into the village for help from M'sieur Lemaître, but I couldn't stay here. The only answer was to hide out in the countryside at the back of the cottage and wait for nightfall. I'd still be taking a chance that the Germans searching the area might find me, but it was the least risky option.

I came down from the attic and looked out of the back windows of the house, to the open countryside. Like much of the countryside around Malerme, the area was flat, but with small patches of woodland dotted about. There was one such wood just across the fields from the back of the house. The problem was getting to it without being spotted. Although there were no Germans in the fields backing on to the cottages, there were plenty of people who might think that selling me out to the Germans would be a way of ensuring their own safety.

I saw that most of the fields were hedged, and drainage ditches had been dug around the edges of the fields by the hedges. Because it was June and the summer had been mainly dry, I hoped the ditches wouldn't be too filled with water, although the bottoms would be sure to be muddy.

I armed myself with a sharp kitchen knife, grabbed some bread, put on my flying jacket and slipped out of the back door. Crouching low, I made it to the first ditch unseen, crawled into it, and then worked my way on my knees and elbows along the network of ditches until I reached the wood. Once there, I set about constructing a place to hide out of branches. It wouldn't protect me from a proper search, but it would keep me hidden from casual glances.

I spent the day in the hide, easing my hunger with pieces of bread. No one came into the wood to search. Occasionally there was shouting from the direction of the village, and all day I could hear the rumble of heavy traffic. I wondered if the Germans were going to try and repair the bridge, and hoped my destruction had been complete. It would be heartbreaking if, after the tragedy of what had happened to Pierre, Berthe and Mimi, the bridge was able to be brought back into use.

I waited until darkness fell, and then made my way through back lanes and ditches to the village. Keeping in the shadows, I made it to the village centre, and the back door of Lemaître's bakery. A light was on in the bakery. I listened, but there were no voices from inside, so I could only hope that he was alone.

I tapped at the door, then retreated to a hiding place in the shadows of an outbuilding.

The back door of the bakery opened, and I saw the figure of M'sieur Lemaître silhouetted against the light. I gave a bird-like call as a signal. Immediately, M'sieur Lemaître opened the door wider, and I hurried to it. I slipped inside, and he shut and locked the door behind me.

"You are still here," he muttered.

"What's happened to Berthe and Mimi?" I asked. "Are they still alive?"

Lemaître nodded.

"Fortunately, the officer in charge decided that Pierre was the only one who might be engaged in Resistance operations. But they are to be sent to a labour camp." He shook his head sadly. "Very few people come out of them alive, I'm afraid. The conditions there are very bad."

"The bridge?" I asked.

For the first time, he smiled.

"Destroyed," he nodded. "Completely." Then his expression grew serious. "You have to return to England. The Gestapo will know about you by now – there is no way Berthe and Mimi will be able to resist their questions."

"I can't leave now! I want to stay here and avenge them," I told him.

Lemaître shook his head.

"You will only make things worse," he said. "Either you will be caught and tortured and give us up, or we'll have to spend valuable time protecting you instead of carrying out acts of sabotage and helping British airmen to get back home. You've done what you came here to do, now you must go back to England. We will avenge the Megris family."

He strode to a large metal ring in the middle of the wooden floor, tugged at it and lifted a trapdoor to reveal a ladder going downwards.

"One of my cellar store rooms," he said. "You will stay here while I get our radio operator to make contact. I shall pile sacks on top of the trapdoor to hide it. Whatever happens, don't leave here."

I nodded and climbed down the ladder. The cellar smelt damp. There were just bits of old machinery down here, nothing that could go mouldy, like flour. Then the trapdoor closed above me, and I was plunged into darkness.

I pulled my flying jacket tight around me, and settled down on the damp floor in the pitch darkness to wait.

Chapter 21

I don't know how long I sat in that darkness. It was certainly several hours, but I had no way of checking the passing of time. When I finally heard the sounds of sacks being moved above me and the trapdoor opening, daylight flooded in, temporarily blinding me.

"A plane is coming for you tonight," said Lemaître. He came down the stairs and handed me a sack. "Here's some food and water for you. You'll have to stay down here today."

"What news?" I asked. "Berthe and Mimi?"

"As I said, they're going to be taken to a labour camp. A lorry is coming for them tomorrow."

I bowed my head.

"I'm so sorry," I said. "I didn't mean for them to suffer."

"They knew the risks when they got involved," said Lemaître.

"Not Mimi," I contradicted him. "She's just ten years old."

"There is no age limit when you are fighting for your country," said Lemaître. "And it wasn't your fault. If Pierre had only kept that temper of his under control …!" He shook his head. "I told him, time and time again: smile to their faces and pretend. That's the way we'll win."

He headed back to the ladder.

"Whatever happens, no noise, and stay here."

He climbed back up the ladder, and once more dropped the trapdoor and covered it with sacks of flour. This time it wasn't as pitch dark in the cellar as before – daylight filtered through the cracks in the floorboards above me, enough for me to see to open the sack for the provisions.

The day I spent in that cellar seemed so much longer than the time I'd spent the previous day, hiding in the wood. For one thing there were the sounds of people moving about upstairs, and the voices, many of them German. The whole time I was on edge, always expecting the trapdoor to be thrown open and to find a bayoneted rifle pointed at me.

The hours passed, and finally the vague shreds of light between the floorboards faded and then vanished as night fell, and once more I was in complete darkness.

I don't know how long I was in that darkness before I once again heard the sounds of sacks being moved, the trapdoor opening. M'sieur Lemaître was standing over the open trapdoor, holding an oil lamp.

"It's time," he whispered.

I climbed out of the cellar and followed him out of the back door of the bakery. His battered old van was waiting there. Sitting inside in the passenger seat was Martin, our look-out from the night of the bridge.

I climbed into the back of the van, and M'sieur Lemaître stacked sacks of flour in front of me to hide me. He slammed the rear doors shut. I heard the driver's door open, then shut; the engine fired up, and we were moving.

As we drove, I thought of the last time I'd made a journey in this van, hidden by sacks of flour in the same way. Then, Pierre had been still alive. Berthe and Mimi had been free. But then, the railway bridge across the Clemel had been intact. Now it was gone.

The van chugged on its way. I wondered who would be coming to pick me up. Would it be the same pilot, Jim? Soon I would be back in England and I could report back to Mr Swinton that the mission had gone as planned. The bridge was gone.

I felt a change in the vibration of the van as we left the road and began to bounce – I guessed we were going across a field. The van stopped. The front doors opened, then the rear doors, and Lemaître hauled sacks away from me so I could scramble out.

Martin was already heading towards the middle of the field, a can in his hand containing petrol to start the fires.

"The plane should be here soon," whispered Lemaître.

We stood there listening, our ears straining for the sound of the small plane's engine; as we did, I heard another noise – an engine, but that of a different vehicle.

Suddenly we were illuminated by strong lights, car

headlights that had suddenly switched been on. Two, three cars were there, their lights picking us out, and also Martin. Shouts in both German and French were ordering us to put our hands up.

"Germans!" yelled Lemaître.

I was terrified. To be so close to getting away, and now this! Would they shoot us?

I saw Martin drop the can he was holding and he began to run, heading for the far side of the field.

BRRRRRRRR!!!!!

An explosion of rapid gunfire from a rifle burst the silence of the night sky, and Martin tumbled to the ground and lay motionless.

There was no chance of us making a run for it. We'd be dead before we'd moved. Reluctantly, Lemaître and I raised our hands above our heads as the German soldiers surrounded us, pointing their rifles at us.

Then I heard it, the sound of the plane's engine approaching and then turning as the pilot saw the car headlights and the scene below. There was the cough of a throttle as the plane quickly changed direction, then the sound of its engine was heading away from us, going back to England. Mission aborted.

We were caught.

Chapter 22

Lemaître and I were handcuffed and bundled into the middle seats of a long car, with two armed soldiers in the rear, and a driver and another armed soldier at the front. The car was one of a convoy of three. I noticed that were weren't heading towards the village, and looked at Lemaître questioningly.

"We are headed for Caen," he said.

"Shut up!" snarled one of the soldiers. "No talking!"

When we reached Caen we were driven into the centre of the town, the convoy pulling up in front of a building hung with a huge swastika flag. We were pulled out of the car and roughly pushed into the building, being jabbed now and then with the rifles to move us more quickly. We were in the hands of the Gestapo.

We were ushered along a corridor to a metal door. This was unlocked and opened, and we found ourselves in what looked like a cell block, containing four cages made of strong metal. Our handcuffs were taken off us and we were pushed into a cage together. The door was slammed shut and locked, and the soldiers left us, locking the metal door behind them.

We looked around the cage. There was nowhere to sit, so we squatted down on the cement floor. None of the other cages were occupied, although there were signs that someone had been in one of them recently. There was dried blood on the floor of it.

Neither of us spoke, but we both knew what the other was thinking. We were in Gestapo HQ. We had been caught red-handed in the field, shortly after the railway bridge had been blown up. We were not going to come out of this alive.

I don't think I've ever felt as bad as I did at that moment. It had broken my heart when Mum was killed, and when I got the letter telling me that Dad was dead, but this … This was happening to me! I was going to be tortured and killed, just as Mr Swinton had warned me. There would be no time for more missions to help beat the Germans, no time to tell Aunt Abbey how much I loved her, and how sorry I was that she'd be left alone without me. I was terrified about what was to happen to me, and completely miserable thinking about Mum, about Dad, about Aunt Abbey, about the War. I felt so overwhelmed by it all that I wanted to burst into tears, but then I determined that I wouldn't give the Germans the satisfaction of seeing me cry, of knowing how scared I was.

There was the sound of a key in the metal door, then it opened and a Gestapo officer entered, accompanied by an armed soldier who trained his rifle on us through the bars of the cage.

"Up!" snapped the soldier.

We got to our feet. The Gestapo officer smirked at us.

"Caught like rats in a trap," he said.

"Who betrayed us?" demanded Lemaître angrily. "Who informed on us?"

"You did," said the Gestapo officer.

Lemaître looked at him, bewildered.

"What do you mean?" he asked angrily.

The officer shook his head, still smiling.

"You thought you were so clever, buttering up our soldiers, giving them presents of pastries and cakes when they came into your shop. But it struck me, how can you do that, M'sieur Lemaître, and yet the villagers do not despise you or spit at you in the street for being friendly with German soldiers. No, they treat you with respect. Why is that? I wondered." He shook his head. "You may have fooled the local officer here, but not me. A few days ago I decided to have you watched. I could have had you picked up and brought in for questioning once I suspected you, but I decided to let you carry on, knowing that sooner or later we'd catch you with some even bigger fish for our haul." He turned his gaze on me. "Like the young lady. Special Operations, I assume? Another one of Winston Churchill's secret army?"

"I am a French citizen," I said defiantly.

The Gestapo officer let out a derisive laugh.

"You really think we are that gullible?" he demanded. "I have spent many hours, days even, interrogating your sort. You think I don't recognize what you are? A spy parachuted in by the English. You are the one who destroyed the bridge."

"My name is Céline LeBlanc and I am a student teacher …," I began, but an angry shout from the officer cut me off.

"Stop this nonsense!" he roared. "I will question you first, young lady. Monsieur Lemaître here can tell me about the local Resistance, but you, young lady, are the key one here. You will tell me about the Special Operations Executive. How it works. Who leads it. Where its training camps are."

My first reaction was shock that he seemed to know so much about the SOE; but then I realized with bitterness that he would know an awful lot. I guessed he'd interrogated captured agents before.

"I'll tell you nothing," I snapped at him.

The Gestapo officer smiled confidently.

"Oh, I think you will," he said.

With that he turned and left the cell block, followed by the soldier. The metal door slammed shut behind him, and we heard the key turn in the lock.

"So, they have brought in Schnell to interrogate us!" muttered Lemaître bitterly

I turned to him, shocked.

"Did you say Schnell?"

Lemaître nodded.

"Sturmscharführer Maximillian Schnell. Head of the Gestapo in Caen. A cruel man."

And the man who killed my father.

....

We sat on the floor of the cage, leaning back against the wall.

"They will have a listening device somewhere in here," whispered Lemaître. "That's how they get most of their information, from listening to prisoners talking amongst themselves."

"Then they will just learn that I am Céline LeBlanc, a student teacher from Rouen."

Lemaître smiled.

"All I can give them is my recipes for bread."

We sat in silence for another twenty minutes or so, then the metal door opened and three soldiers came into the cell block. While two of them kept their rifles aimed at Lemaître, the third ordered me out of the cage and handcuffed my wrists behind my back. The cage was locked behind me, and I was escorted out of the cell block and along the corridor to a door. I was pushed into a room where Schnell was waiting, standing by some shelves examining some nasty-looking tools and weapons.

At the sight of them, and the sight of Schnell standing there with an evil smile on his face, I nearly fainted from fear at the thought of what was about to happen to me. I couldn't speak for fear of my teeth chattering with terror.

The room was otherwise bare, except for a table and two heavy-looking wooden chairs. There were no windows, just a shaded light bulb.

"Put her in the chair," ordered Schnell.

The soldiers pushed me down onto the chair, pulling my arms behind me, and I felt my handcuffs released, then felt them bite into my skin as they were snapped shut again, this time fixing my wrists firmly to the wooden strut at the back of the chair.

Please, let me die soon, I prayed silently. Don't let me suffer the pain of torture!

Schnell walked away from the shelves and sat down on a chair facing me.

"In this room I have a variety of instruments at my disposal," he said, gesturing at the shelves. "All manner of things to cause you great pain." He leaned towards me. "Some people say that the worst thing of all is the fear of these instruments. Thinking about the pain they will cause." He leaned back. "Personally, I disagree. The pain is far worse." He smiled again, a vicious smile. "I'm going to let you think about what is going to happen to you tomorrow morning, if you don't answer my questions." He gestured at the terrifying objects on the shelves again. "Look at them, Miss Céline LeBlanc, as you call yourself, and think of them being used on you. You will save yourself a lot of agony if you tell me what I need to know now.

"Where is the Special Operations Executive based? In London. Elsewhere?"

If I talked, I would be saved from the pain. Or would I? I didn't trust this man or anything he said. This was the man who'd killed my father. Even if I told him everything, I knew he'd kill me.

My mouth felt dry with fear, but I forced myself to look directly into his face and say: "My name is Céline LeBlanc and I am a teacher visiting relatives."

Schnell ignored what I'd said and continued, his voice low, almost friendly in tone.

"How were you recruited? How many agents are in SOE? What is your real name? Where did you receive your training? Who was your contact before you came to France?"

"My name is Céline LeBlanc and I am a student teacher visiting relatives," I repeated.

Schnell sat, watching me quizzically. Then he said: "Very well, if that is how you wish to play it. So let's try this the other way. You will spend tonight in your cage, thinking about what you will endure from tomorrow morning. And I can assure you, it will be very unpleasant."

Chapter 23

I didn't expect to sleep that night, but I did. Despite the fact that there was just a bare, hard concrete floor, and I was threatened with the most painful torture the next day, I fell asleep. Maybe it was the fact that I'd had so little sleep for the past few days, or perhaps being captured had stopped the adrenalin pumping that had kept me going while I'd been in France. Whatever the reason, I found myself being shaken awake in the morning. My first feeling was fear surging through me: it was time to be questioned by Schnell. But then I became aware of the sounds of sirens and alarms and lots of shouting in German. It was Mr Lemaître who was shaking me, and I was bewildered to see that he had a broad smile on his face.

"What's happening?" I asked.

"The invasion!" burst out Lemaître, his voiced filled with triumph. "I've been listening to them shouting! The British and the Americans have landed on the Normandy beaches! The Germans are in a panic! It is the end of the War!"

"Invasion?" I asked, bewildered.

Lemaître nodded.

"It is what we have been hoping for for so long! The Allies on French soil – thousands and thousands of them, with tanks and heavy weapons! At last! They will crush the Germans and push them all the way out of France and right back to Germany, and there they will smash them for good!" He took my hands in his. "If we get out of this alive, remember this day, ma chérie! The 6th of June 1944. The day of our liberation. The day of our deliverance!"

There was a rattling of a key in the metal door, and then it swung open to reveal two armed German soldiers, and another with a bunch of keys. While the other two pointed their rifles at us, the one with the keys unlocked the door of the cage. He pointed at me.

"Come with us!" he snapped.

"Why?" I asked.

"The Sturmscharführer orders it."

No! I thought. This can't be! He can't still be intending to torture me, not with this happening!

"No!" burst out Lemaître. "The war is over! The Allies are here! What is the point of torturing and killing her now?"

"The Sturmscharführer orders her to be brought to him," repeated the soldier. He jerked his finger at me. "Come!"

"No!" I refused.

"If you do not, we will shoot him," he said, pointing to Jules Lemaître.

I sighed and stood up.

"They would have taken me anyway," I said ruefully to Lemaître.

I walked out of the cage. The soldier slammed the door shut and locked it again.

"Come!" he commanded, and the two soldiers jerked their rifles menacingly at me.

I followed the soldier, the other two bringing up the rear, their rifles clutched firmly in their hands. I couldn't believe it! Surely Schnell would not start questioning me now, not with the invasion happening!

The general office of Gestapo HQ was in a state of semi-panic. All the uniformed men seemed to be rushing to clear out cupboards and desks and empty their contents into metal waste bins.

"Destroy everything! Leave no evidence!" barked a voice from an outer room, which I recognized as belonging to Schnell. Then the Gestapo officer strode into the general office.

"Good!" he said, satisfied, when he saw me. "Put her in my car. And put handcuffs on her. We can't take chances."

The soldiers handcuffed me, then ushered me out of the building to where the Sturmscharführer's car was waiting, his driver standing beside it. There were two flags flying on the front wings to identify it as that of a high-ranking SS officer: one a swastika, the other the double lightning flashes which made up the letters SS. The soldiers pushed me into the back seat of the car, then stood back to await the arrival of Schnell, their eyes on me the whole time.

What was going on? Where was Schnell taking me? And why?

After a few minutes, Schnell appeared carrying a bulky briefcase. He snapped an order to his driver, who saluted and got behind the wheel of the car, starting it up.

Schnell turned to the waiting soldiers.

"Make sure all paperwork is destroyed," he ordered. "There must be no evidence left." With that he raised his arm in salute, barked "Heil Hitler", and then got into the back of the car next to me.

As the car moved off, I demanded: "Where are you taking me?"

My voice must have betrayed my fear. I was confused and very scared.

"Somewhere I can question you without the threat of interruption," said Schnell.

"But the Allies have invaded. The War is over!" I burst out.

I felt an overwhelming sense of bewilderment and rage. Everyone else would be saved when our soldiers got to Caen, but I was being taken away by Schnell. Away from any chance of rescue.

"The War is not over," growled Schnell. "Our forces will hold them off and then force them back into the sea. But there is the danger of air attacks in this part of Normandy, and I don't want to risk losing such a valuable asset." He gave a smirk. "In this situation, your information will be extra valuable."

"If you keep me alive, you can use me to trade when the Allies catch up with you," I suggested, desperate to stay alive: "My life for yours."

Schnell shook his head.

"No," he said. "I don't want you giving evidence against me. All I need is what you know. Then I will kill you."

....

Schnell's car headed south on the main road out of Caen, but our progress was soon hampered by columns of tanks and armoured cars heading north, towards the invasion.

"This is taking too long!" Schnell barked at his driver. "Take the road by the river."

The driver turned off the main road and cut through a series of side roads until he came to a smaller one which ran alongside a narrow river. There were some German vehicles using this road heading towards the coast, mainly lorries and buses filled with troops, but when they saw the two flags fluttering on the wings of our car, they pulled over to let us pass. We made much better time on this road, and soon we were clear of the advancing German vehicles and racing along.

Suddenly I was aware of the driver saying nervously: "Sturmscharführer …"

We both turned to look at the driver, and saw through the windscreen that an RAF fighter plane was coming in very low, directly towards us. Suddenly bullets began to hit the road in front of the car, and then the windscreen smashed and the driver fell to one side with a dreadful gurgle. I had anticipated what was happening and had thrown myself down to the floor, the plane's bullets whizzing over my head and smashing the glass of the rear window.

The car swerved wildly. I felt it leave the road, bounce over the rough ground, and then smash into a tree with such force that turned it over. I fell towards the side of the car as it slid onto its side, then we hit something else and the car rolled completely over onto its roof.

The impact made the doors fall open and I fell out onto the grass, and just managed to stop myself from rolling down the grassy slope into the river. The driver of the car was half-in half-out of the car, dead. I could only guess that the pilot had spotted the two flags on the front of the car, realized there was a high-ranking German officer it, and gone for the kill.

I stumbled to my feet, hampered by the fact that my wrists were still handcuffed behind me. I looked around for Schnell, and saw that he had fallen out of the car. He'd been hit – blood soaked the front of his shirt.

"Help me!" he whimpered.

Unsteadily, he raised a hand towards me in appeal, then he fell back with a groan.

As I saw him lying there, semi-conscious, I thought of all the people he had killed and the cruel way he'd done it. Not just my father, but all those others who'd been dragged into that dreadful interrogation room and been subjected to unspeakable torments. Hundreds of them had suffered at the hands of this monster, and then been killed by him. I thought of Aunt Berthe and little Mimi. Of the hundreds of other people this man had tortured and killed.

Then I realized that he wasn't breathing any longer.

He was dead.

Epilogue

The keys to the handcuffs were in Schnell's pocket, as were the keys to his briefcase. Inside the briefcase were masses of documents, diagrams, maps and plans. The German language lessons I'd received during my training helped me translate some, enough to know that they contained vital information. All I had to do was get them back to England. The question was: how? To the north there was fierce fighting as the invading Allies battled to break through the German lines. Elsewhere, there was a sense of chaos, with German troops torn between retreating south and holding their lines.

It was the invasion, M'sieur Lemaître had said: the Allies landing in force on the beaches of Normandy and forcing their way inland, liberating France as they went. So I decided to wait for the Allies to arrive.

As it turned out, fortune came my way and I didn't have to wait for the Allies. After I left Schnell and his wrecked car, I took a chance and sought refuge with a family on their farm, telling them I was a refugee from the north who was waiting for the fighting to die down so that I could rejoin my family. Luckily for me, they were part of a Resistance cell. The sight of Schnell's bulky briefcase raised their suspicions, and I found myself being interrogated as a possible spy or collaborator by the local Resistance commander. Fortunately, by taking him to where I'd left Schnell's body, and also mentioning the events at Malerme – though without naming names – I was able to convince him I was on their side, and arrangements were made to get me back to England.

....

So it was that a week after I'd blown up the bridge over the Clemel, I was back in Edward Swinton's office. I'd been delivered by car straight to Baker Street after I'd landed at Tempsford, still clutching Schnell's briefcase.

Swinton nodded approvingly as he studied the contents of the briefcase.

"Excellent catch!" he said. "This is a real bonus! There's information here that will be absolutely invaluable to us." He smiled at me. "And that was an excellent job, the bridge at Clemel. It did exactly what we hoped, stopped the Germans being able to get reinforcements and heavy weapons to the coast along that rail line." Then his expression grew serious. "Unfortunately, the invasion isn't the end of it. There's a long haul yet before the War is over. But the tide has turned because of it." He paused, the said: "We might have need of you again, if you are willing."

I thought about all that had happened to me while I was in France. Being captured and threatened with torture and death. Pierre being shot dead. Berthe and Mimi being transported off to an unknown fate.

And then I thought of everyone who'd died trying to defeat the Nazis. People who'd sacrificed their homes, their families, their lives. After five long years, we were close to victory now. With a last push, we could win!

"Very willing," I said.

"Good," he said. "In the meantime, I think we'd better get you cleaned up and returned home. I know your Aunt Abbey will be curious to hear all about your secretarial work, and why it's kept you away from home."

"I'll tell her it's classified," I said.

And so I got myself washed and cleaned up and, dressed in my own clothes, became Violet Debuchy once more, and went home to my Aunt Abbey.

"You missed all the excitement!" burst out Aunt Abbey. "The Allies have landed in Normandy! They say the War will be over any time now!" She sighed. "Ah, the bravery of those soldiers! We're so lucky, Violet, being women. We don't have to suffer like men do in this war. The fighting! The shooting! The explosions!"

I looked at Aunt Abbey and thought of everything that

had happened to me. The SOE training. France. Pierre, and Berthe and Mimi. Schnell.

"You're right, Aunt Abbey," I said. "But we all play our parts, you know. Even us."

Historical Note

It took another six months after the D-Day landings in Normandy, on 6 June 1944, before the whole of France was liberated. The war in Europe carried on for a further five months before Germany finally surrendered on 7 May 1945.

The Special Operations Executive (SOE) was known as Churchill's Secret Army. It operated in countries occupied by the Axis forces (Germany, Italy and Japan). Its largest area of operations was in Occupied France. Between May 1941 and August 1944, more than 400 SOE agents were sent into France, including 39 women agents. Of these, 91 men and 13 women were killed. Of those who survived the War, many had been caught, tortured and imprisoned in the notorious death camps, before being liberated.

On May 1991, a memorial was unveiled at Valençay, a small town in the Loire Valley in France, with the names of the 91 men and 13 women of SOE who gave their lives to gain France's freedom. In October 2009, a memorial to SOE's agents was unveiled in London, on the Albert Embankment by Lambeth Palace. The sacrifice of those who fought this secret war against the Nazis was finally recognized. Without their bravery, there would have been no victory.